Sanction Blue

By
Robert Fisher

Sanction Blue

Copyright © 2018 Robert Fisher
ISBN: 978-1-7320865-6-2
Library of Congress Control Number: 2018956864

The main protagonists in this novel are fiction. Any similarity to persons living or dead is coincidental. Of the actual historical individuals mentioned, every effort had been made to keep their words, intentions and actions consistent with recorded history. The endeavor was to follow chronological events as they relate to the narrative.

La Maison Publishing, Inc.
Vero Beach, Florida
The Hibiscus City
www.lamaisonpublishing.com

Chapter 1
The Acquirer

The Army truck drove swiftly through the moonlit night carrying its important cargo across the seemingly endless expanse of the Nevada desert. The cab was silent, save for music from the radio and the muffled hum of the engine.

"Man, this blows," complained Private Munch, who sat in the passenger seat across from Sergeant Parker.

Sergeant Parker looked at him. "I like this song," he said jokingly, though he knew what Munch really meant.

"It's not the song, man. When I joined up, I expected to see some action. Instead, I get assigned to guard duty at China Lake and now I'm transporting guns. I want action!" answered Munch.

Parker smiled, remembering that he had once said the same thing years ago.

"Son, trust me – this is paradise compared to what I saw over there. No one's shooting at you and you're not surrounded by blood and death," said Parker.

"Yeah, but I want excitement and action. Hell, I feel like a glorified UPS driver," complained Munch.

"We all make a difference in our own way. After all, it's not all explosions and shootouts," Parker reminded him.

"Fine, but this is still boring," grunted Munch.

"Better to be bored than dead," responded Parker, who was starting to get annoyed with Munch's whining.

Parker turned his head back to the road and was surprised to see a van blocking it. A man ahead waved at the convoy. "What the hell is this?" asked Parker.

Munch looked up from the radio. "Must have broken down," he observed.

"Damn, this is gonna make us late," grunted Parker. He stopped the truck, stepped out, and walked over to the man standing by the car.

Instinctively he studied the man's appearance. He was a tall, muscular-looking man dressed in a black trench coat, dress shirt with a tie, and pants with a silver belt. His face was ordinary and plain with brown eyes. On his head was a black fedora with a wide brim and a gray band. He wore gray gloves.

"What seems to be the problem, sir?" the sergeant asked politely.

"Thank God, someone finally stopped to help me," said the man. "I hope I'm not slowing you down."

"No trouble at all. Now then, what seems to be the problem with the van?" asked the sergeant, a little annoyed.

"I don't know. One minute I was driving; the next it just stalled. Can you help?" pleaded the man.

"Maybe it's the engine. Pop the hood," said the sergeant. When the man did, Parker leaned over to investigate.

Behind him, the man pulled out a silenced Glock 19, and shot once Sergeant Parker in the back of the head.

"Oh, shit!" exclaimed Munch. He jumped out of the car as he reached for his pistol. However, before Munch could pull the trigger, he fell over dead, smoke wafting out of a bullet hole in the back of his head.

Slowly, another man walked onto the road from the side holding a still-smoking sniper rifle. "All too easy," he said to the man by the car.

"Good shot, Misha," said the man in black. He holstered his gun, pulled out a phone, dialed a number, and started talking.

"Mr. Zero, this is Counselor Black. Phase one of Project: Big Picture is complete."

He hung up and helped Misha take the gun cases out of the truck and put them in the van. Once they were done and all the crates were in the van, they got inside and drove away into the distance.

Chapter 2
Into the Shadows

There is a hidden world beyond the curtain of the world we know. Glimpses of it are seen in the news, and countless stories take place in it. It is a world of spies, arms dealers, assassins, and black operations. It exists at the intersection of organized crime, espionage, and terrorism. If it had a name, the most fitting would be the Shadow World. One of the denizens of that world – General Mark Connors, who spent his entire military and intelligence career living in it.

Before he became a four-star general, Connors fought for his country in the mud and blood of the Vietnam War as a Green Beret. In the years after the war, he took part in several covert operations around the world for the Central Intelligence Agency. Years later, Connors was appointed by the president to be the new leader of the most secretive division of the CIA, a division so enigmatic and powerful that only its Director, Connors, and two other people in the entire American government were aware of its existence. Sometimes, in their most private moments, they wished they weren't.

Officially, the CIA is divided into four groups: The Intelligence Division, National Clandestine Service, Science and Technology Division, and the Support Division. However, there is a secret fifth Division known as Silhouette, or by its code name: Sil 5.

Silhouette's purpose is to covertly eliminate any and all enemies of the United States of America by any means necessary, regardless of the law. Every major intelligence agency in every country on earth has an organization like it, covertly operating outside of the law, whether they admit it or not. While there is no official name for these kinds of intelligence organizations, those in the corridors of power refer to them as "shadow agencies."

It was morning at the CIA's headquarters in Langley, Virginia, known as the George

Bush Center for Intelligence. General Connors had just arrived. He was a tall man dressed in a dark green blazer, black tie, white shirt and dark green pants, his black hair graying with age. Connors walked through the doors of the lobby, which had the CIA's logo emblazoned on the floor. After going through security, he went straight to the cafeteria and bought the first of what would be many cups of coffee.

He then went to his office on the second floor of the sprawling complex. He greeted his secretary, Janet, and then placed his hand on the thumbprint scanner, which served as the lock for his office. As soon as the door opened, he walked inside, closed the door behind him, and sat down at his desk.

All in all, it was a typical morning for him. At least it would be if he didn't have to see his visitors. He looked at his watch.

They are probably already here, he thought. As if on cue, the phone rang. He picked it up, gave his authorization code, and listened to the scrambled voice on the other end.

"Yes, sir, understood; I'll be there immediately," Connors said.

Connors took a big gulp of coffee and wished he were drinking something stronger. He placed the coffee on his desk, stood up, and walked toward a bookcase on the left side of the wall. He pulled a book off the shelf entitled *Birds of the West Indies* by a certain British author and opened it to page 107.

The center of every page after 107 was removed to make room for a thumbprint scanner. Connors placed his finger on the scanner; ACCESS GRANTED appeared on the scanner screen.

The bookcase slid to the right, revealing an elevator, which led directly to Silhouette's top-secret headquarters code named THE BRICK, located under the CIA's campus. Connors closed the book and placed it back on the bookcase.

The general straightened his tie before stepping inside the elevator, pushing a button marked CONFERENCE ROOM. "Dammit! How could this have happened?" muttered Connors under his breath as the doors closed in front of him.

When they opened, Connors was standing in Silhouette's conference room. On the wall across the room was a screen, in front of which was a long conference table. Seated at the head of the table was the president; on his left was the Director of the CIA; on his right was the Secretary of Defense. In one room – the only three other people in the entire US government aware of Silhouette's existence.

Although Silhouette was a division of the CIA, they answered directly to the president, which had always irked the CIA director. Connors took a seat next to the Secretary of Defense.

The president scanned the room. "Gentlemen, I understand that we have a problem," he said casually.

The Director of the CIA stood up, walked towards the screen, pulled a remote out of his pocket, and aimed it at the screen. Instantly, an image of the army truck appeared on the screen.

"Seventy-two hours ago, an army truck carrying several experimental, next generation rifles were hijacked en route to a testing facility," said the director.

"This might be a dumb question, but how are a few stolen M16s a Silhouette problem?" asked the Secretary of Defense.

"Just the tip of the iceberg," muttered Connors.

The president looked at Connors quizzically.

"'Something you want to add General?" asked the president.

"Yes, sir. Those weapons are part of Project: Ironhide," answered Connors.

"General, that's classified," barked the director.

"Shut up, David, you and I both know how serious this is – the president has a right to know," said Connors angrily. "Sir, may I continue?" He shifted his attention to the president.

The president nodded. The CIA Director shot Connors a dirty look, which he ignored.

"Thank you, sir, Project: Ironhide was initiated by Silhouette and funded and implemented by our front company, Twilight Industries. The intention of the project was to develop state-of-the-art weapons and tech for our operatives … and ultimately, for the military," he explained.

"So how did these people get them?" asked the president.

"We are working on that, but based on their tactics, the organization that's responsible is highly trained and precise," said the CIA director.

"Highly trained and precise? Please tell me you know more than that!" said the president nervously.

"Sir, we have several suspects," the director replied.

"Go on," the president gestured.

"Well, our primary suspects are the Heise She li Triad, Vasilev Syndicate, and Rojas Cartel," said the director.

"It's not them," interrupted Connors.

"Excuse me?" said the director.

"It's not them, Neither the Triad, Vasilev or the Rojas cartel knew about that facility or the weapons, and even if they did they would have gone about it differently," Connors said. "My point being, this was too clean for Vasilev and the Triad" explained Connors.

Connors frowned as he continued. "In fact, I think this hijacking was a small part of some bigger scheme and frankly, sir, recovering those guns is impossible. I suggest we figure out who stole them and stop whatever it is they took them for."

The president leaned back in his chair and thought for a minute before speaking. "Could this be connected to that civil war in Belarus?"

"No, sir, we've been monitoring that extensively since it began, and it seems to be contained within their borders," replied Connors.

"What about another shadow agency? Could they be behind it?" asked the secretary of defense.

Over the years, Silhouette had come into conflict with or worked with other shadow agencies. Connors knew it was possible that one of them was the culprit; however, it was impossible to know which one. "It's possible," Connors shrugged.

"Do you have any ideas on how to handle this, General Connors?" asked the president.

"Yes, give me permission to reactivate and deploy ECHO 9 and have them track down who stole the weapons, and stop whatever it is they're planning."

"All right, Connors, since your agency has the expertise – not to mention that it's your fault to begin with – you're going to handle it by any means necessary," said the president. "Consider this permission to reactivate ECHO 9."

"Sir, I must protest! Silhouette has plenty of other agents that could handle this," said the CIA director.

"His guns, his problem, his way of dealing with it. Incidentally, I'm shutting down Project: Ironhide, effective immediately. If this gets out of control, the last thing we need is for the press to discover it," said the president as he and the secretary of defense stood up and left.

The director looked at Connors grudgingly. "The ball's in your court, Mark. Try not to fuck up," he said.

"You mean like you did?" asked Connors sarcastically.

The CIA Director scowled at Connors in anger as he left.

Connors got in the elevator and returned to his office. Once he was in his office, he took a sip of coffee and then spit it out.

"Damn, its cold," muttered Connors. Tossing the cup in the garbage, he called Janet for a new cup of coffee and leaned back in his chair.

Janet brought him a fresh cup of coffee, leaving as quickly as she entered.

Connors took a big gulp, before logging in to the computer and bringing up the file marked ECHO 9. He began reading. He already knew most of it since he had put the unit together, assigning its missions.

ECHO 9 was the code name for a unit that carried out covert missions for Silhouette. Like all of Silhouette's field agents, they were taken from the best of the best of each branch of the Special Forces and Intelligence Communities. As a result, it was the most efficient, covert, and deadliest group of warriors on the planet.

However, five years after its formation, the president ordered the team disavowed. Its members were discharged from the military and Silhouette. ECHO 9 was shut down; its three surviving members returned to civilian life.

Connors skipped to the team bios section. Since all former Silhouette employees were kept under heavy surveillance by Silhouette's Internal Affairs branch – Blacklist Protocol – the files were up to date. The team leader was the most important for tactical purposes. Connors started there: ECHO 9's field leader, Simon Kane. He began reading.

Captain Simon Kane

AKA: Simon Dio Kane

Birthplace: Long Branch, New Jersey

Code name: MONOLITH

Height: Six feet and one inch

Eyes: Green; right eye lost in an accident and covered by a black eye patch

Current age: 35

Former SEAL Team Six operator and ECHO 9 field leader

Current location: Jensen Beach, Florida

Current occupation: Freelance security

The information continued in detail: *As per standard Silhouette training, Simon Kane is proficient in all NATO and Warsaw Pact firearms and proficient in multiple forms of martial arts. He can drive multiple types of military and civilian vehicles, and is an expert at disguise and subterfuge as well as intelligence collection. Extremely dangerous, he is currently under heavy surveillance.*

Captain Kane is proficient in German, Russian, Spanish, French, Italian, Portuguese, Mandarin, Cantonese, Japanese, and Arabic.

Note: Ex-Husband of Agent Sheila Goodbody (Code name: LITHIUM).

Connors looked at Simon's picture; he was a clean-shaven man with black, slicked back hair, and a black eye patch over his right eye while his left eye was green. He had a rugged yet handsome face, and at least in the photo, a slight tan as a result of his time in the Middle East.

"He probably still has that damn trench coat," muttered Connors. He clicked on the notes section and began to read.

In the mid 1980's Simon Kane's father, Thomas Kane, a former member of the Australian SASR (Special Air Service Regiment) immigrated to the United States. He met Maria Dio, an Italian American history teacher at Shore Regional High School in Long Branch New Jersey. Eventually they married and had one son (Simon Kane). Shortly after Simon graduated from Shore

Regional High School, they were killed in a car accident. After graduating from Rutgers University, Simon Kane joined the US. Navy where he eventually became a member of the Sea Air and Land teams (SEALs).

After serving with the SEALs for several years, he was accepted into the Naval Special Warfare Development Group code named SEAL Team Six and became its Captain.

In his second year in SEAL Team Six, while on a mission to capture an Iraqi HVT, he was caught in an explosion which cost him the use of his right eye. During the mission, his team was wiped out, but he managed to survive long enough to be rescued by a Ranger team that was deployed to provide evacuation and support to the team. Captain Kane was taken to the US Army hospital near Ramstein, Germany so he could be treated and recuperate.

The doctors managed to remove the burns across the right side of his face via plastic surgery. His right eye could not be saved and had to be amputated. He covers the wound with a black eye patch.

Connors skipped the next few lines, which contained mostly medical jargon and continued reading.

During his recovery, he was recruited into Silhouette by its director, General Mark Connors, and underwent Silhouette training at the Central Intelligence Agencies training facility at Camp Peary (code named The Farm), CIA University and THE BRICK. When his training was complete, he became the field leader of ECHO 9 (see ECHO 9).

Connors skipped to the final paragraph.

Five years before ECHO 9 was decommissioned, Simon, and the teams CIA/SAD representative: Agent Sheila Goodbody became romantically involved and ultimately married. However, when ECHO 9 was decommissioned and its operatives were discharged, Simon and Sheila divorced (possible cause: domestic abuse incident involving Simon's alcoholism; not certain).Sheila moved to Seattle and became a writer; Simon moved to Jensen Beach, Florida.

Connors scrolled down and read about his current activities.

Simon Kane currently works as a freelance bodyguard/security contractor. Every Saturday he goes to a local gun range and puts several magazines of rounds through his pistol, a Jericho 941, for which he has a concealed carry license. Accuracy is not diminished. Exercises promptly at

6:30 *every morning using the exercise regimen he learned in SEAL team Six. Sober since the divorce.*

Connors scrolled to the next page, which contained Sheila's information.

Agent Sheila Minos Goodbody
Birthplace: Philadelphia, Pennsylvania
Code name: LITHIUM
Height: Five feet, three inches
Eyes: Brown
Current age: 35
ECHO 9s/Silhouettes representative to the CIA
Former Delta Force and CIA/SAD/SOG operative
Current location: Seattle, Washington
Current occupation: Author
As per standard Silhouette training Sheila is proficient in all NATO and Warsaw Pact firearms and proficient in multiple forms of martial arts. She is able to drive multiple types of military and civilian vehicles. An expert at disguise, Shelia is good at subterfuge as well as intelligence collection. She is extremely dangerous and currently under heavy surveillance.

Agent Goodbody is proficient in German, Russian, Spanish, French, Italian, Portuguese, Japanese, Arabic, and Chinese languages.

Note: Ex-wife of Captain Simon Kane

Connors turned to the notes section of her file.

After returning home to Philadelphia from the Vietnam War, Ajax Minos, a first generation Greek-American, met and married Ada Goodbody, a half-Irish, half-French, doctor working there. Due to her mother's death from complications during childbirth, Sheila was raised by her father, but she later took her mother's name to honor her memory. After her graduation from the University of Pennsylvania, her father died from alcohol poisoning. Sheila decided to follow in her father's footsteps by joining the army. Eventually she was accepted into the US. Army's Special Forces Operational Detachment-Delta, commonly referred to as Delta Force.

After numerous successful missions with Delta Force, Sheila joined the CIA's Special Activities Division where she did several missions for the Special Operations Group (SOG) as a field agent. She excelled at infiltration, analysis, and extracting information from enemy targets. Eventually she was recruited into Silhouette and became the CIA's representative to Silhouette. It is believed that due to her father's life long battle with alcoholism and death, she refuses to drink alcohol.

Connors skipped the next few lines because they were about her marriage to Simon; he didn't feel like reliving that episode. Instead, he scrolled down and read up on her current activities.

After her divorce, Sheila moved to Seattle, Washington, where she became a fiction writer. Currently, her novel is in the process of being made into a major motion picture. She was recently called the next Tom Clancy by Time *magazine. She has led a mostly reclusive life at her home outside Seattle. Occasionally, she will go to the local gun range and practice with her Walther P99. She has been spotted at a local gym exercising using for several hours.*

Connors looked at Sheila's photo. She had slightly olive skin and short blonde hair that stopped at her shoulders, round glasses, which made her look like an academic – just for the look, he remembered. Perfect vision. Her rather attractive features hid the surly personality he remembered. In the photo, she was wearing a black leather jacket, black t-shirt, and white pants, her "uniform" of sorts.

While all ECHO 9 agents were generally hardened by combat she had one of the most abrasive, stubborn and no nonsense personalities he had ever seen.

She's gonna be the hardest to recruit, thought Connors. Then again, he mused, if Simon could get her to fall in love with him, he could definitely get her back in the field.

He flipped to the third and final member bio.

Sergeant Deon Bowman
Birthplace: San Francisco, California
Code name: ROUNDABOUT
Height: Six feet, five inches
Eyes: Brown
Current age: 35
Former Marine Force Recon commando
ECHO 9s sharpshooter
Current location: San Francisco, California
Current occupation: Car mechanic

As per standard Silhouette training, Agent Bowman is proficient in all NATO and Warsaw Pact firearms and multiple forms of martial arts. He can drive multiple types of military and civilian vehicles and is an expert at disguise and subterfuge as well as intelligence collection. He is extremely dangerous and currently under heavy surveillance.

Sergeant Bowman is proficient in German, Russian, Spanish, French, Italian, Portuguese, Japanese, Arabic, and Chinese languages.

Notes: Has been arrested for being in several bar brawls.

Connors chuckled. *He hasn't changed a bit.* Deon was brought into Silhouette and by extension, ECHO 9, just like Simon and Sheila. Connors scrolled down the page. On the last page something caught his eye.

Deon is currently working as a car mechanic in San Francisco; suspected to be doing part-time work for the American branch of the Chinese Heise She li Triad. He is frequently seen at a nightclub run by a member of the aforementioned criminal organization.

He looked at Deon's picture – a tall, muscular black man with short black hair. Connors put the folder down and pressed the button on his desk that connected him to his secretary.

"Janet, put me on the first flight to Palm Beach International Airport and make sure someone is there to meet me," Connors said.

"Yes, sir," responded Janet over the phone.

Connors leaned back in his chair. "This should be good," he said to himself.

Chapter 3
The Man with One Eye

Connors' driver pulled into a parking spot across the street from a park. Connors stepped out of the car and looked at his bodyguard.

"Stay in the car," Connors told his bodyguard, code-named KRYPTONITE.

"Sir, what if he kills you?" asked KRYPTONITE.

"He won't," Connors answered evenly.

"How do you know?" asked KRYPTONITE.

"Because he hasn't done it since we got here," replied Connors.

He walked across the street, into the park and sat down on a bench next to a pathway. He sat there before a man in a dark blue trench coat with an eye patch where his right eye used to be. Then walked up behind the bench and sat down next to him.

Simon Kane looked slightly older than Connors remembered. "It's hot out today," said Connors.

"But not as hot as Asbury Park," replied the man next to him.

"Hello, Simon," Connors said.

"Save it; you've got five minutes before I'm gone," Simon said angrily.

"Nice to see you, too, Simon. And by the way, how's the eye?" Connors asked.

"Still gone," replied Simon dryly.

"Listen, I'm reactivating ECHO 9 and I need your help," Connors said.

Simon's expression didn't change. "Assuming I'm interested, why are you getting the band back together – cat stuck in a tree?" he said.

"Several days ago a shipment of state-of-the-art rifles was stolen by an unknown, highly trained organization. We want you and what remains of ECHO 9 to find out what they were stolen for," said Connors.

"Send someone else." Simon pulled a toothpick out of his pocket and put it in his mouth.

"I need the best of the best for this. Besides, all of Silhouette's other agents are busy," replied Connors.

"That's bullshit," Simon said calmly. "You only want us to do it because we're expendable, Connors." Simon turned and glared at Connors. "Well, fuck you! After you shut down my team, I lost my will, my sanity, and the only woman I ever loved!" barked Simon.

Connors shrugged. Simon was right, at least from his perspective. "So I'm guessing the answer is no?" he asked sarcastically.

"Quick as ever, Connors," snapped Simon.

"Be that as it may, seeing Sheila again might give you a chance to …."

"I wouldn't finish that sentence if I were you," growled Simon.

Connors grinned slyly. "Or what? You'll kill me? Go ahead! But know that if you do, every single intelligence agency and law enforcement agency in this country will be on your one-eyed ass, and when they find you they will gut you like a fish," Connors said.

"And besides we both know that you need this," continued Connors.

"What the hell are you talking about?" Simon asked angrily.

"Don't bullshit a bullshitter, Simon. People like us don't just retire and return to civilian life. Admit it; you miss the life." Connors paused. "Incidentally, here's another reason to do it: God only knows what those people plan on doing with those guns."

"Your point?" asked Simon.

"Can you live with the knowledge that you could have stopped them and saved lives but chose not to?" Connors asked, knowing the answer. So I repeat, are you in or not?"

Simon thought back to the events of the last year and knew Connors was right. He did indeed miss the life. *Maybe this* would *give me a chance to patch things up with Sheila,* he thought.

"You're right, goddammit. Fine, I'll do it," said Simon.

"Good, I knew you'd see things my way." Connors stood up. He reached into his pocket, pulled out an airplane ticket, and handed it to Simon. "Which is why I took the liberty of procuring this," said Connors.

Simon looked at the ticket, confused. "San Francisco?" he asked.

"That's where Deon is, not to mention our only lead on the theft," Connors explained.

"After you've checked out that lead, head to Seattle to recruit Sheila personally," continued Connors.

Simon stood as well. "What makes you think I can get her to sign on for this?" Simon asked.

"Because you know how she thinks," Connors stated the obvious.

Simon rolled his eyes. "Fine, but how the hell am I supposed to find Deon once I get there?" asked Simon.

"He's already in, he'll meet you at the airport" replied Connors.

"And Sheila?" asked Simon.

Connors handed Simon a slip of paper. "Here's her address; she's a writer in Seattle" said Connors.

"She any good?" Simon asked as he read the address.

"She's okay" Connors answered. "The bad guy in the book has an eye patch."

Simon raised his eyebrow. "I wonder where she got *that* idea" he replied.

Connors turned to leave, calling back to Simon over his shoulder. "Your flight leaves tomorrow. Good luck" said Connors.

Simon shrugged, as if luck would have little to do with anything. He put the papers in his pocket and walked back to his Chevy El Camino. As Simon drove back to his apartment in Jensen Beach, he thought about what Connors said, particularly about Sheila. They'd been divorced for a year and hadn't seen each other since then.

Getting discharged from Silhouette had not been good for their marriage. Meeting there, they'd clicked immediately, eventually gotten married, and stayed married for four years – until the work ended forcing them to return to civilian life. Finding it hard to adjust to civilian life, Simon sought refuge in a bottle. He became consumed by it, leading to the divorce. Sheila's departure was definitely a wake-up call for him; he got sober – but he couldn't bring himself to talk to her again. She hadn't contacted him since she left so he just decided to let it go.

When Simon arrived at his apartment, he walked inside and went straight to his bedroom, opened his closet, and knelt down in front of the safe there. He typed in the combination. When it beeped and opened, he reached inside, pulled out a small rectangular wooden box, and closed the safe.

Very deliberately, he closed the closed door, and sat down on his bed. Only then did he open the box. Taped on the inside of the lid was a picture of Simon and Sheila in Hawaii, smiling. "Happy Anniversary, Simon" was written on it. Simon smiled at the picture of the loving couple.

Simon dug through some papers to get to the bottom of the box, which held a custom IMI .40 SW caliber Jericho 941. To the left of the gun was a small box of ammunition and two magazines, a total of eight rounds. *Only Sheila would give someone a pistol for an anniversary present.* Simon checked the gun over. Ever since he lost his eye in the Iraq war, this had been his weapon of choice; it had been the perfect gift. Just looking at it brought back memories of his time in Silhouette and of Sheila.

Chapter 4
Bayside Reunion

Following a decent flight, Simon Kane's plane landed at San Francisco International Airport. After getting his luggage at baggage claim, he walked outside and was about to hail a taxi when he heard a familiar voice behind him. "Anyone ever say that you look like a pirate with that eye patch?"

Simon smiled knowing exactly who that strong yet laid back voice belonged to. He turned around with to see a very tall, African-American man dressed in black pants and a yellow t-shirt. He had a muscular body with a strong looking face and thin black hair. Smirking, he held a black briefcase in his left hand. "Anyone ever tell you that you have really bad taste in shirts?" replied Simon sardonically.

"Says you." replied Deon.

Simon was pleased to see that Deon hadn't changed.

"Nice to see you, Deon," Simon said as they shook hands.

"How you been, brotha?" Deon asked.

"Surviving, you?" answered Simon.

"The same," replied Deon.

Simon asked, "Where are you parked?"

Deon pointed to the closest parking lot. "Over there."

"Lead on" replied Simon drily.

Simon followed Deon out of the airport to the parking lot where his car waited.

Simon was surprised to see Deon's car, a dark green 1968 Ford Mustang. "I don't believe it – you still drive that piece of shit!" laughed Simon.

"Fuck off. This car is a classic, just like the one in *Bullitt*," replied Deon.

"Why couldn't you drive a car from a *good* movie?" Simon put his bag in the back seat.

"Do you wanna walk there, One Eye?" Deon replied.

"Not exactly … but I could use some exercise," Simon said as they both got into the front seat.

The two former spies glared at each other for several seconds then laughed.

"Anyway, what's with the briefcase?" asked Simon.

"Connors sent it over in advance," Deon said as he handed the briefcase to Simon.

Inside there was a dossier marked *Kranz*. What caught Simon's eye, though, was the syringe and small bottle next to it.

"He hasn't changed," muttered Simon as he closed the briefcase.

"The more things change, the more they stay the same," Deon said dryly as the engine growled to life.

Deon dodged cabs and cars as he made it back onto the highway.

"Did Connors brief you?" Simon asked.

"Yep," Deon answered. "And I gotta tell ya, I'm glad to be back in the game."

"After everything Connors pulled, you still like the life?" Simon asked.

"Hell yeah, man! I've always loved the action, and thrills of the life and so do you," Deon said.

"Yeah, I guess you're right. If I'm being honest, part of me was thrilled when Connors called," Simon said, admiring the skyline out the window.

"Still, it carries a heavy price," continued Simon.

"Hey man, you've got to let what happened between you and Sheila go," Deon said. "It's been two years since the divorce. I'm sure she isn't *still* mad at you."

"And what are you basing that well-thought-out conclusion on?" Simon asked sarcastically.

Deon shrugged his shoulders. "Wishful thinking?" he replied.

"Works for me," Simon said dismissively.

"Anyway, it's been like a year since ECHO 9 was shut down? What have you been up to?" Deon asked.

"After Sheila … well, after I sold our house, I moved to Florida, rented an apartment. Other than that nothing, except for the occasional security job," answered Simon. "What about you?" asked Simon.

"I came back here and took over the family mechanic shop," answered Deon.

Simon squelched a laugh. When they were in ECHO 9, Deon Bowman was perhaps the most dangerous sniper on the planet, not to mention an extremely dangerous hand-to-hand combatant and expert mechanic. Now he was a car mechanic.

Simon looked at Deon skeptically.

"Come *on*, there is no way in hell you're just a car mechanic. Hell, I have personally seen you fight five Russian Spetsnaz commandos at once with your bare hands. And *win*!" said Simon.

Deon smiled slyly, "Yeah, Montenegro was fun, still you got me. I sometimes moonlight as a bouncer for this club in Chinatown. Not to mention the occasional bar fight," answered Deon.

The Mustang rounded a turn and slowed down as they pulled into the parking lot of Deon's shop. "Well, here we are," Deon said, driving into the rear garage.

"Downstairs is the shop," said Deon, as they walked up the stairs to his apartment.

"And this is home" said Deon as he turned the key.

It was a typical bachelor pad. On the kitchen counter was a pizza box from

California Pizza Kitchen. Simon looked inside and grimaced at the slice inside.

"What?" Deon asked.

"Pineapple on pizza. It's just not right," Simon said, shaking his head disapprovingly.

Deon laughed. "Seriously, man, try it!" said Deon.

"If I did, my mother would roll over in her grave," Simon said.

Deon laughed, picking up a shirt thrown over the couch back. "Anyway, sorry about the mess," said Deon.

"Don't worry about it; my place looks even worse." Simon said, sitting on the couch.

"I'll bet," Deon muttered. He walked into the kitchen, returned with two open beers, and sat down in the chair across from Simon.

Simon saw the cold bottles in his hands and tried to keep his eye off of it. It brought back bad memories. He studied the room until Deon noticed.

"Sorry, Simon, I forgot you were in recovery," Deon said apologetically. He took the bottle from Simon and set it on the coffee table.

"I'm not, not anymore. Seriously, don't worry about it. After Sheila left, I quit the stuff. I haven't touched alcohol in a year," Simon said.

"Glad to hear it, man, more for me" said Deon.

"That's all ancient history. Connors said something about a lead here in Frisco?" Simon was grateful to be talking about the job, and not himself.

"According to the dossier his name is Rudolph Kranz. He's a freelance thief, apparently hired to infiltrate the base and find out about the convoy. After the job he was spotted landing at San Francisco International airport," explained Deon. "Then ... poof! Gone like a fart in the wind," Deon said as he held out his hand and opened it.

Simon grinned at the analogy. "Great, so how do we find him?" he asked.

"That is where I come in, remember that club I told you about?" said Deon. When Simon nodded, he continued.

"It just so happens to be run by the Heise She Li triad," explained Deon.

"So?" Simon asked.

"If you want to get out of the country from San Francisco without being seen, the Heise She li Triad is who you go to," answered Deon.

"And he'll help us because …?" Simon asked.

Deon explained, "Fortunately for us, the local kingpin owes me a few favors."

Simon would have loved to hear the story, but decided to save it for later.

"So when do we go see him?" he asked.

"Tonight," Deon said solemnly. "I called him this morning and set up the meeting."

Chapter 5
Death and Taxes

During the day, the streets of Chinatown are littered with vendors and stores selling food and curios. Much later into the night, the sidewalks are mostly barren, the stores closed with metal gates on the doors and windows. But the lights of Chinatown glitter brightly, driving away the darkness.

The town was awash in the light of luminous multilingual signs adorning the buildings as Deon and Simon made their way to the rendezvous point. Suspended between the buildings, high above the road, hung glowing paper lanterns that bathed the area in faint red hues.

Simon and Deon drove down the main street. Making a hard left at the first intersection, they arrived at their destination: the Chinese nightclub known as The Red Castle.

A large four-story building constructed of red brick, its name was emblazoned in vivid red neon on the front in both Chinese and English characters. On the roof rested a large red decorative pagoda giving it the look of an ancient castle. In front, were four stairs; at the top stood a Chinese man in a red vest, white dress shirt, black tie and pants, standing authoritatively behind a podium.

"Guess they took the name literally," Simon said, taking it all in as they pulled into the parking lot next to the club. It was a cool enough evening that Simon was dressed in his dark blue trench coat, under which he wore a white dress shirt, black pants, and tie that Deon had loaned him. Deon was wearing a white blazer with a light blue dress shirt and black pants.

Simon followed Deon to the man at the podium who looked up casually from what he had been doing. "Ah Mr. Bowman, welcome to the Red Castle! Follow me, please," the host said politely.

They nodded and followed him inside. The interior was bathed in dim blue overhead lighting. In the center of the room was a large dance floor with people dancing wildly to the loud music pervading the room. Simon and Deon followed the host to a door at the far end of the club. Standing imperiously in front of the door was a large muscular Chinese man in a black suit. The host walked up to him and whispered a few words in his ear in Mandarin.

The man looked at them deductively, then stepped aside and opened the door for them.

"He's waiting for you in his office on the top floor," said the host.

Simon and Deon walked through the door as it closed behind him, reducing the blaring music to a muffled whisper.

"Well, that was ominous," Simon said sarcastically as they walked up the four flights of stairs.

Reaching the top floor, they walked into a plush, upscale lobby. A guard stood in front of the only door. Imposing though he seemed, his tone was casual. "I have to frisk you before you enter," he said.

"Big surprise," muttered Simon.

The man patted them down and removed their guns from their shoulder holsters. "It's a dangerous neighborhood," Deon said with a cocky smile.

Not amused by Deon's flippant remark, the guard placed their pistols in his pocket, and opened the door.

Sitting behind an ornate and oversized desk was Mr. Bai, the renowned leader of the Triad. Short, older, and slightly corpulent, the balding Chinese man in a suit and wizened features still managed to exude power.

"Ahhh...welcome back Mr. Bowman. Please sit down." Bai was suspicious about the man with him.

"Who is your friend?" asked Bai.

"He's an old friend of mine," Deon said as they sat down in front of the desk.

Bai grinned. "I like to know the names of the people I do business with. I find I live longer that way."

"Call me MONOLITH," Simon answered with a whiff of nostalgia as he uttered his old code name.

"Excellent! Now that we have exchanged formalities, gentlemen, let's get down to business," said Bai calmly.

"We're looking for a guy named Rudolph Kranz. Do you know him?" Deon asked.

Bai wagged his head back and forth slightly. "I know of a German by that name, he came here asking for our help to get out of the country and for sanctuary. It seems that his employers wish to wrap up any loose ends. Naturally we agreed to hide him … at least until he runs out of money." Bai appeared to be quite happy with the arrangement.

"Out of curiosity, I would like to know what your interest in Mr. Kranz is?" continued Bai.

"Does it matter?" Simon asked.

"Not in the slightest," replied Bai.

"Do you have any idea who might have hired him?" Simon asked.

Bai thought for a few moments, the wheels in his mind turning. "There is only one organization brazen enough to hire someone like him to infiltrate one of your weapons labs like he did," said Bai.

Simon and Deon exchanged a glance, deciding without a word not to ask how he knew about the weapons lab. "And this organization is …?" Simon sounded slightly annoyed.

"They call themselves the Networc, with a 'c,'" said Bai.

Simon and Deon locked eyes once more, confused. During their time with Silhouette, they had become familiar with a wide variety of criminal and terrorist organizations. They had never heard of an organization called the Networc.

"Who or what is the Networc?" Deon asked.

"Most of the people I have heard speaking of it think of the organization as a myth. Me and my superiors do not agree. All I know about them is that their reach is global and their resources are seemingly infinite," said Bai.

"They sound like Bond villains," Simon muttered.

"That's putting it mildly. Since they have designs on Asia – *our* territory – we're enemies," said Bai.

"Still you didn't answer my question. Why do you want Kranz?" asked Bai.

"He owes us taxes," Simon said as Deon muffled a snicker.

Bai shrugged. He certainly understood the concept and he owed Deon.

"Fine then, you can have him. We in the Triad despise the Networc. A chance to stick it to them is too good to pass up," replied Bai as he rubbed his hands together.

"Still ... we have expended a lot of money and resources in hiding him. To make sure we have not wasted that money and resources, we would need some ... compensation," said Bai.

Deon pulled a check out of his coat pocket and placed it on the desk. Bai picked it up, looked at it and smiled slyly.

"Yes, this should more than cover it." He studied the check, holding it up to the light. "One question – what does Twilight Industries have to do with this?" He tapped the signature on the check.

"It's a long story," answered Simon.

Bai waved his hands, already late for another appointment. "It usually is. Mr. Kranz will be at Pier 22 at the docks at 1:30 in the morning. I assume you'll want him alive?" asked Bai.

"And unharmed," Simon answered.

"Of course … well here's a good place where you can talk to him about his 'taxes,'" said Bai as he wrote down an address and handed it to Deon.

"Thank you," Deon said. As the shook hands with the Triad leader, Bai handed Simon his business card.

"Mr. MONOLITH, if you are ever in San Francisco again ... or in China ... look us up. Any friend of Deon's is a friend of ours," said Bai casually.

"Thanks," Simon said with a fake smile. He put the card in his wallet, hoping he would never need to use it.

Deon and Simon walked out of the office and back down the stairs. "Some friends, Deon," Simon said.

"Hey, they come in handy," replied Deon.

When their guns were returned at the ground level, they were slightly surprised to find that they had been cleaned.

*****

Located at the port of San Francisco, the docks serve as a hub for shipping and commerce. Usually they are a hub of activity, but tonight they were oddly quiet and desolate. Next to the harbor were seemingly endless rows of warehouses, the walkways between them lit by dim streetlights.

Finding Pier 22, Simon and Deon sat in the car, anxiously awaiting their quarry like hunters. The quiet cloak of the night made the pier perfect for an underworld handover.

Stakeouts and waiting did not come naturally to men such as Deon and Simon. The omnipresent, all-encompassing quiet, not to mention the boredom, made such tasks almost unbearable. Still, compared to what they were prepared to do to Kranz for his crimes, they would rather wait. Although skilled at their profession, they had never treated the act of inflicting violence with pleasure.

As they sat in the car they talked and played cards until suddenly Deon's phone rang; he had a text message from an unknown number with only the words *two minutes*. Deon showed the screen to Simon, who nodded in silent understanding. After all, this was not the first time they had done a job like this.

"Hand me the Taser in the glove compartment," Deon asked quietly.

When Simon did so, he prepared it for firing. They got out of the car and took cover as the lights of a vehicle approached.

It was a black SUV. The passenger door opened and Kranz stepped out. The car immediately backed up, turned around, and drove away as Kranz's face went from surprise to terror; he turned around at their approaching footsteps.

"Who ... who's there?" asked Kranz nervously.

Deon aimed the Taser at him and fired, causing Kranz's whole body to jump. He fell to the ground writhing and shaking until finally, he passed out. Deon holstered the Taser and they picked him up, handcuffed him, and tossed him in the trunk of the car, then drove away into the inky black night. An hour later, they arrived at their destination, a rundown warehouse on the other side of the harbor.

Two Triad guards greeted them.

"Follow me," said one of the guards as he ushered them in.

Simon and Deon followed him inside while dragging the still unconscious Kranz into the warehouse. Simon made sure to bring the briefcase. As they followed the man, they saw several guards above them on the catwalks. At the other side of the warehouse, the guard pulled out his phone, aimed it at the wall, and pressed a button. Instantly a section of the wall slid away, revealing a flight of stairs that led to the basement.

They followed him down the stairs into the cold basement and down a hallway until they reached a door at the end of the hallway.

"Everything you need is in there," said the guard pointing to the door. "If you need anything we'll be upstairs." He left quietly.

Simon and Deon looked at each other in silent agreement about their next course of action. They looked down at their quarry, pulled him into the room, and closed the door. Inside the small space was a wooden table, a chair, a bucket of water, and two black ski masks.

Donning the masks, they handcuffed Kranz to a chair, and threw water in his face to wake him up.

"Where am I? Who are you?" groaned Kranz.

"Mr. Kranz. It's time to pay your taxes," Simon said.

Chapter 6
Blood and Thunder

"Mr. Kranz we can do this the easy way or the hard way; the choice is entirely up to you," Simon said.

"Personally? I'd pick the easy way," Deon said.

Kranz glared at both of them coldly, the hatred in his eyes burning brightly.

"Well, which is it? Easy or hard?" Simon taunted.

"Do you really think that I'm afraid of you? Or of your tortures?" said Kranz defiantly.

Simon and Deon looked at each other and sighed. "I guess it's the hard way then," Deon said.

The two returned their gaze to Kranz. "Mr. Kranz, you have made two huge mistakes,"

Simon said, turning away to walk toward the table.

"What?!" Kranz eyed Deon as he took a position behind him.

"The first is that you took that job in the first place," Simon said as he opened the briefcase.

Suddenly Deon grabbed Kranz's head and held it steady. Despite his struggling, he couldn't free himself from Deon's iron grip.

"The second is that you assumed we would have to resort to torture to make you talk." Simon removed the syringe and bottle from the briefcase, filling the syringe with liquid from the bottle. He held it and pointed up, his thumb on the plunger as he approached Kranz.

There were many names for the compound in the syringe. Every shadow agency had developed and used some variant of it over the years. This particular variant was known as Compound 1138; most simply referred to it as Truth Serum. It had been developed internally by Silhouette using resources from Twilight Industries during the Cold War at a cost of $5 million. Over the years, Silhouette had developed certain protocols regarding the serum's use. Despite having certain unfortunate side effects. It remained a controversial tool in the organization's toolbox.

While skilled in multiple methods of interrogation, ECHO 9's members had used it themselves over the years for certain missions. For others, they relied on more hands-on methods of interrogation.

Kranz's eyes were full of fear, locked onto the syringe as Simon drew nearer. Simon ignored him as he plunged the syringe into his neck and pressed down on the plunger. Simon and Deon stepped back as Kranz's head fell forward.

Every fiber of their beings was repulsed by this, but there was no time for other methods. *This will save lives*, they told themselves, trying not to think about what it would do to Kranz.

Suddenly Kranz's body tensed up and quivered. His eyes went wide.

"I forgot about this part," Deon said as he looked away in disgust.

"I wish I could," Simon muttered.

Kranz arched his back, then went limp again, and looked up with glassy eyes as if in a trance.

"Let's get this over with," Deon said.

"What is your name?" Simon asked clearly and concisely.

"Rudolph Kranz," Kranz answered softly and distantly.

"Where were you born?" Simon continued.

"Frankfurt, Germany," said Kranz.

Kranz had answered both test questions correctly; Simon decided to get to the point. "Who hired you to find out when the weapons from China Lake would be transferred?"

Kranz's face was blank. "I was hired by Imran Nadella to infiltrate the base and gather intel," he answered.

"Who is Imran Nadella?" Simon asked.

Kranz's expression did not change as he said, "He is a top member of the Networc."

Suddenly, before they could pursue the matter further, they heard a loud explosion upstairs, followed by gunshots.

"What the hell was that?" yelled Deon as he pulled out his 9mm Beretta and cocked it.

"Nothing good," Simon said dryly as he pulled out his Jericho.

"Stay here. I'll go check," said Simon as he cocked the pistol.

Deon nodded in understanding.

Simon tossed his mask on the ground, since it would obstruct his vision as he ran upstairs. When he reached the landing he could see five guards, guns drawn, hiding behind the giant open doors shooting at several gunmen outside. With a glance, he took in the AK-47s, Uzis, M4 carbine rifles, and various automatic pistols.

The gunmen, dressed in black with anti-riot masks, were armed with mostly Glock 17 pistols and what appeared to be H&K mp5 submachine guns and M4 carbine rifles, along with various automatic pistols.

Simon ran over to the nearest group of Triad guards and knelt down next to them. "What the hell's going on?" he hissed.

"These guys showed up out of nowhere and fired an RPG at us," replied the guard frantically.

Simon leaned out of cover and peered at the attackers. Based on appearances and weapons they likely weren't with any local criminal syndicate. Simon leaned back behind cover. Leaning just out of cover, he aimed his pistol at one of the attackers and fired, hitting him in the head. Switching to another gunman, he fired two shots, hitting his target in the shoulder and neck, before darting back behind cover.

Breathe. He leaned back out and fired two more rounds, killing one and injuring another.

"Shit, been outta practice too long," Simon muttered to himself.

"ROUNDABOUT, we are under attack. Have to move Kranz, over," yelled Simon into his earpiece.

"Roger that, over," Deon's voice came back clearly.

As Simon put the radio back, he assessed the situation outside. The injured man grabbed his bleeding shoulder as he ran to the back of a car and pulled out a grenade launcher. In seconds, it was aimed inside.

"Shit! Scatter!" yelled Simon. He jumped behind a row of shipping crates just before the man fired.

The resultant explosion tossed the guards around like confetti. Most of the guards were dead; some lay on the ground whimpering in pain. All who could were shooting, though dazed. Simon leaned out from cover just in time to see one of the guards machine get machine-gunned to death as he attempted to crawl to safety. Simon leaned back, waiting to see if the attackers would enter the building. Sure enough, thinking they had won, one of the attackers walked right past Simon.

Simon grabbed him from behind and wrapped his right arm around his neck, turning the man into a human shield. With his left arm, he grabbed his machine gun and fired a short burst at the other attackers, killing three of them.

Return fire from the attackers took out his "shield." Simon dropped the man, ran behind the shipping crates while shooting, and slowly began working his way towards the door. As he did so, he called Deon again on his radio.

"ROUNDABOUT, get Kranz and let's get out of here, over," Simon spoke quietly.

"Way ahead of you, MONOLITH," responded Deon.

A steely voice barked behind Simon. "Stop, bastard!" Simon turned to face one of the gunmen; an Mp5 was aimed right at him. Suddenly, there was a loud bang as the gunman's head flew back; he fell on his back, dead.

Whipping around, Simon was relieved to see Deon, smoke still wafting from his gun's barrel. Kranz stood in an unsteady stupor behind him, still handcuffed.

"Nice shot. Although you were cutting it kind of close weren't you?" Simon said.

"Close enough," replied Deon sarcastically.

Simon looked back at the dead body and then back at Deon.

"Too close for my taste – let's get out of here!" Simon barked.

Pulling Kranz between them, they ran outside through a side door at the end of the warehouse, across the rear parking lot, and to their waiting car. Just as they were about to maneuver Kranz into the back seat, he suddenly fell over, blood pouring from a bullet wound in the back of his neck.

"Shit!" barked Simon angrily.

"Get in, dammit!" yelled Deon, who peeled out in a hail of gunfire.

"Who the hell were those guys?" Simon asked once they were out of range.

"My guess is they were agents of this Networc group that Kranz was talking about, trying to shut him up," Deon said.

Simon's eyes narrowed. "Real question is … how did they know where to find us?"

As though in answer, Deon's phone rang.

Deon glanced at the number and mouthed the name *Bai* before putting the phone on speaker.

"Are you two okay?" asked Bai.

"Yeah, we had a little run-in with some party crashers," Deon said.

"How did they know where to find us Bai?" Simon asked. The accusation in his tone was evident, though understated.

"Mr. MONOLITH, just because you are a friend of Mr. Bowman does not mean you can talk to me however you wish," Bai reminded patiently.

"But to answer your question, we have identified a Networc spy in my office. This spy has already been dealt with … harshly. Take this as a lesson. The Networc has people everywhere. Oh, and Deon, do not worry about your car. We will repair it and return it to you. Good day, gentlemen," said Bai. He hung up.

"Well, at least the Mustang will be alright," Deon said.

"Oh thank god, I was so worried" Simon replied sarcastically while brushing some glass fragments off his shoulder. Bullets had shattered the rear window completely, with stray shots on all of the others.

"So let me guess – we're off to Seattle to pick up Sheila?" Deon asked.

"Damn right, but before we go I'm gonna call Connors and ask for any intel. on this Imran Nadella guy and the Networc," Simon replied. He leaned his head back. "And I could use a shower."

Chapter 7
Lithium Flower

On the late afternoon flight from San Francisco to Seattle, Deon watched a movie. Simon was lost in thought, telling himself he needed to relive the events in the warehouse when what he was doing was avoiding thoughts of a reunion with Sheila. *What will she say when she sees me? Probably an insult, but more important ... what should I say? "Hi Hon, sorry I didn't call in two years. How are you, by the way want to go on a mission?"*

Usually Simon was in a hurry to get to his target destination; today, though, he wouldn't mind a few delays.

Sheila was unique among women in the military and in Silhouette. Only a handful had met the qualifications for membership in Silhouette, perhaps as a result of her time in Delta Force. She possessed a fierce no-

nonsense attitude and an unwavering stubborn will in addition to deadly combat skills. To this day, Simon wondered what a talented, beautiful woman like her had ever seen in him. *And how did she make me fall in love with her? I wasn't looking for love.* Simon looked out the window at the clouds covering the earth like a blanket.

"Hey, Simon, how are we gonna get her to agree to do this?" Deon nudged him, taking out the airplane earphones.

Simon looked away from the clouds at Deon, trying to come up with an answer. "The same way Connors got us to agree to do this – by confronting her with the truth."

"I don't know … she's settled into civilian life pretty well. Hell, she's a bestselling author now! And she's not half bad," responded Deon.

Simon was surprised. "You read her book? What's it called?"

"*The Action Hero Squad.* It's about mercenaries fighting terrorists, kinda like *James Bond* meets the *Fast and Furious* movies," Deon explained.

"*The Action Hero Squad*? The title needs work," Simon said raising an eyebrow.

"Eh, I've heard worse," Deon shrugged, "but I heard they're making a *movie* out of it. I wonder who'll play me?" He chuckled.

"Anyway, what did Connors say? I think I dozed off while you were telling me last night."

Simon leaned over closer so they couldn't be overheard.

"Apparently this Nadella guy is a Saudi billionaire. He's hosting a big party at his mansion in Monaco this weekend," said Simon.

"And we're gonna crash it?" Deon asked.

"Someone has to," answered Simon.

"What about those guys that attacked us at the warehouse. And the Networc?" asked Deon.

"Connors couldn't find anything on the Networc or on those guys from the warehouse, but they were definitely ex-military from the look of them," answered Simon.

A melodic voice came over the intercom. "Ladies and gentlemen, please fasten your seat belts securely and place your tray tables in the upright position in preparation for landing. Welcome to the Seattle-Tacoma International Airport. We hope you enjoy your stay!"

Simon looked out the window as the city slowly rushed up to greet them. After landing, they walked outside and were about to hail a taxi when a black car pulled up in front of them. A man in a black suit stepped out of the driver's side.

"Good evening Mr. Kane, Mr. Bowman, I was sent here from the local office of Twilight Industries to deliver your car," said the man politely, gesturing to the open door.

Simon grinned slyly upon hearing the name of Silhouette's multinational dummy corporation.

Deon looked at the car and studied it. "Damn, I hate Buicks," grunted Deon.

"Good, then I'll drive," Simon said as they got in.

As they edged into the flow of airport traffic, Deon rolled down the window and called to the man in black. "Yo! Elwood Blues!

Next time send a good car!" The man grinned before walking away.

Simon shook his head at Deon as he rolled the window back up.

"What?" Deon asked.

"Are you done?" Simon asked sarcastically.

"Are you?" replied Deon.

Simon shrugged and merged into the correct lane. *No more delays.* He stepped on the gas and they sped off to the Sheila's home. It was dark by the time they reached Sheila's upscale house located in a small neighborhood outside of the city. As they pulled up, Simon saw that the lights were on. The manicured lawn was freshly cut.

"Stay in the car; I want to do this myself," Simon said.

Deon laughed and threw up his hands in surrender. "Hey man, go ahead! No way in hell am I gonna get between *you* two. Just tell me where you want the body sent," said Deon.

"What makes you think there won't be *two*?" replied Simon sarcastically as he got out of the car.

Simon walked slowly and cautiously to the front door, knowing full well that she probably already knew they were there. As he walked across the lawn, he looked at the neighboring houses. Stereotypical suburban homes full of families living happy, blissful lives, ignorant of all the darkness in the world. If they hadn't gotten divorced ... *Could this have been our life together?*

"*Hell* no" mumbled Simon. As much as he hated to admit it, Connors was right: *People like us don't just retire.* He sure hoped Sheila felt that way, too.

Standing in a little covered doorway, he knocked. It felt like a year passed before the door opened and Sheila stood there.

She was dressed in a sleeveless t-shirt and jeans. Her body hadn't changed over the years, still as beautiful and curvaceous as Simon remembered. All those powerful muscles were camouflaged by a lean bosomy figure. Her blonde hair stopped just at her shoulders. Simon could tell she had been following her Army fitness training – curves or no, her arms were well defined. His eyes moved to her face, which had a surly and displeased look he'd seen many times. *Same rugged personality or holding a grudge?* What sounded like music echoed from inside the house.

Simon flashed a grin. "Long time no see, hon. May I come in?" he asked.

In response, Sheila punched him hard across his face so fast he couldn't duck.

Over the years, Simon had been hit many times, by many different people, with varying degrees of pain. This blow hurt more than any of them. Instinctively he put his hand to his cheek.

"I'm guessing that's a no," Simon said as he looked back at her.

"Good guess," Sheila said as she prepared to slam the door. Before it closed, Simon grabbed the door and leaned in close.

"You didn't answer my question," Simon said, mustering cocky smile.

They stared at each other sternly for several seconds. "Ten minutes," Sheila said curtly as she opened the door.

"More than enough time," grunted Simon, moving his jaw this way and that to regain feeling.

Simon followed Sheila into the hardwood-floored living room. There was a light brown couch, complemented by two chairs. The fireplace dominated the room with several tastefully framed pictures over the mantle.

A doorway on the other side of the living room led to Sheila's office, the source of the music he'd heard. As they walked in, he recognized the song and the band: *I Fought the Law* by The Clash. Her taste in music hadn't changed, apparently, still a devoted fan of classic punk rock. Despite the tension, he chuckled softly.

"What's so funny?" Sheila turned to face him accusingly.

"It's kind of ironic, don't you think?" Simon asked. "That song and our old profession?"

"Screw you, it helps me think," Sheila said dismissively, walking over to a large window.

Joining her, Simon saw that it overlooked a flower garden. The moonlight revealed vibrant colors and creative design.

"I never figured you for a gardener," he said.

"Everybody needs a hobby," replied Sheila, feigning disinterest.

The walls of her office were decorated with vintage posters for The Clash, The Ramones, Blondie, and Joan Jett. In the center was a wooden desk. In front, were two swivel chairs; behind it was a leather swivel chair and a floor-to-ceiling wooden bookcase that was filled with books. Even a cursory glance revealed her name on several of the visible spines.

Sheila's desk was well organized, implying her military training; in the middle was her laptop computer, with a speaker from which Joe Strummer sang. Sheila sat down behind her desk, turned off the music, and leaned back in her chair.

She crossed her arms and put her feet on her desk, staring at Simon.

Simon sat in front of her desk feeling like a kid summoned to the principal's office.

"Nice place," he said in an effort to break the ice.

"The clock is ticking, Simon," Sheila said coldly.

She's sizing me up. Simon sighed. At least she retained her skills.

"Connors reactivated ECHO 9, what's left of it, after terrorists hijacked top-secret guns from a military convoy," he explained.

"Stop!" interrupted Sheila. She took her feet down and leaned in. "I'm guessing that he wants to get the band back together and go after the bad guys, right?"

"Pretty much, yeah," Simon said, leaning back in the chair.

Sheila shook her head. "Not interested, I'm done with all of that."

"Bull," Simon smirked. "You know as well as I do that no matter how hard we try, people like us can never live a 'normal' life ... at some level, you miss it."

"What's there to miss?" Sheila's eyes were dark, but he detected a glint of interest behind the mask.

Simon smiled. "The adventure, the excitement. Why, hell – it's the reason you write books like *The Action Hero Squad*. It allows you to reenact the old days," he answered.

"Prove it," grunted Sheila stubbornly.

With lightning speed, Simon reached for his gun. Before he could pull the pistol out of his shoulder holster, he heard the undeniable, all-too-familiar sound of a gun being cocked. He turned and saw that he was looking down the barrel of Sheila's Walther P99. He smiled slyly, knowing he was right.

"I knew it," he said softly. "The training, the instinct – they never go away. People like us don't retire. We only *get* retired," continued Simon.

Gently, Sheila laid the pistol on her desk. "So … are you in?" asked Simon.

Admitting he'd struck a nerve did not sit well with her. "Congratulations, Simon, you were right. Do you want a medal?" Sheila said irritably.

"Do you have one?" Simon asked.

For a brief second, Sheila cracked a smile, but it disappeared immediately. "What makes you think you deserve one?"

Simon was beginning to tire of being Sheila's punching bag. He decided to ask her the question that he'd been asking himself over and over again.

"Was being married to me really that bad?" Simon asked bluntly.

"The anniversary in Hawaii, our honeymoon in Key West, you and me working and living together – so far I'm starting to think it was," Simon said.

Sheila was silent. Of course, they had had good times together, plenty of them and she knew it.

Sheila sighed as she stood up. "Simon, do you even know why I left you?" she asked.

"Because of the drinking," Simon said mournfully.

"No, because of what it turned you into," answered Sheila as she walked over to the window and looked at the garden again.

"You never knew my father but he was an alcoholic. Every night he came home from the bar fall-down, stinking drunk," Sheila explained.

Sheila fought back the tears as her eyes started to bubble over. "He was a Marine in Vietnam, Simon. He was a good man, a hell of a father, *and* a goddamn war hero. The booze turned him into a broken shell of a man," continued Silhouette.

Simon dropped his head but said nothing.

"When we were discharged, I was overjoyed at the possibility of a normal life with you and when you got lost in that bottle, I couldn't witness another man I loved go through that hell again," Sheila said.

"I know you must be angry with me for never telling you why ... for leaving ... but you understand now, right?" she asked.

Though she tried to hide it, there was a rare vulnerability in her voice. Simon walked over to her and held her gently. They were quiet for several seconds, trying to process everything.

Simon had always wondered why she left him. He'd had his suspicions, of course, but now that he knew her story, it all made sense.

"Sheila," Simon murmured, pulling her a little closer, still hesitant.

She looked up, curious, hesitant as well.

"You need to know that I'm not angry with you for leaving ... if anything I'm angry with myself," Simon said quietly.

"Why?" Sheila asked, somewhat surprised.

"Because of my momentary weakness, I ruined the good thing we had," Simon said.

"All this time I thought the spark just went out for you. Even after you left and after I quit drinking, I never once stopped loving you," said Simon.

"Neither did I," Sheila said quietly.

Eyes locked, they each tried to think of what to do next. There wasn't a training manual for this kind of thing. As their words sank in, they smiled, and pulled each other closer.

"Y'know, I always thought those honeypot missions we ran were why you left me," Simon joked.

Sheila smiled and laughed a little. *I've missed that smile,* Simon thought.

"Yeah, that Cuban chick in Miami was really something," Sheila said slyly.

"So I've heard," replied Simon. They moved apart, still a little stunned.

"So ... what now?" Sheila asked.

"Well...You didn't answer my question earlier. About the mission. Are you in?" Simon asked.

Sheila looked out to her garden, mentally comparing her boring middle class lifestyle with the adventure and excitement she'd known with Silhouette. She was still in excellent physical condition. She thought about everything Simon had told her about the mission. When she looked back at him, her cocky smile had returned.

"When do we leave?" she asked.

Simon grinned, immensely satisfied with her answer.

"Tonight. Deon's waiting outside to take us to the airport. We're flying into France, then driving to Monaco," Simon explained.

Sheila's eyes widened. "Deon Bowman? I haven't seen him since ECHO 9 was shut down. How is he?" she asked.

"Well, you know Deon," replied Simon dryly. "Still driving that shit car of his."

Sheila laughed. "We haven't changed a bit, have we? None of us."

"Not even a little," Simon said.

Sheila picked up her pistol. "I'm going to get packed," said Sheila.

Simon followed her out of the office, across the living room and eventually to the door to her bedroom, where she stopped him.

"Wait here," Sheila said.

"Seriously?" Simon asked drily. *Just like that, the armor is back on*

"You heard me," Sheila said firmly. She stepped into the bedroom, closing the door behind her.

"Right," Simon muttered, shifting his attention to the living room.

As he waited, Simon walked over to the fireplace to study the pictures more closely. Their anniversary picture was in a frame beside her medals; there were a few photos of her at book signings.

Simon lifted the anniversary picture and studied it. The happy couple stood on the beach; in the distant background were the forest-covered mountains of Hawaii. Simon wore an orange and green Hawaiian shirt and swim trunks; Sheila was in a white, sand-covered dress with a red flower in her hair. His arm was around her shoulder; hers was at his waist. *Can it ever be like that again?*

"I always hated that shirt," Sheila said gently behind him.

Simon turned around. He had been so focused on the picture that he hadn't heard her come in. She was dressed in a black t-shirt, black leather jacket, white pants, and boots. One hand grasped the handle of the same rolling suitcase he'd seen for years.

"Seriously, a one-eyed piece of Jersey trash like you has the worst taste in clothes," Sheila said with a smile.

"That's funny, coming from someone who dresses like a Hell's Angel," retorted Simon.

"Whatever, One Eye," Sheila said dismissively as she shifted her attention to the picture.

Simon smiled at hearing her favorite insult for him. He replaced the photo and they both stood looking at it for a few seconds, remembering the old days.

"What does all this mean for us?" questioned Sheila.

"I don't know, but let's take it slow, at least until this thing for Connors is wrapped up. We still have a lot to talk about," Simon answered her.

"Works for me" said Sheila.

They turned and walked to the front door. They both reached for the handle, looking at each other in acknowledgment that something had been rekindled deep inside them.

Deon looked up from his book just as Simon and Sheila walked out of the house and towards the car. He had slid over to the driver's side.

"No way," muttered Deon, shaking his head with a little smile. He popped the trunk and got out of the car to greet Sheila with a hug.

"Hey Sheila, how's it going?"

"Nowhere fast," replied Sheila sarcastically.

Simon put her suitcase in the car before getting in the front passenger seat while Sheila got in the back. Deon started the car.

"Well, boys and girls, let's rock it!" Deon said as he put the car in reverse and stepped on the gas.

Chapter 8
Party Planning

The flight to Nice, France, was long but uneventful. Once they arrived at the airport, a representative of Twilight Industries greeted them at and escorted them to a waiting car.

"Too bad there's not an airport in Monte Carlo," Simon sighed.

Twilight Industries kept a local office in Monte Carlo – in reality, a front company for Silhouette that developed there equipment and provided them with their funding. They followed the driver into the garden-variety office lobby with couches, tables, a fountain in the center.

At the receptionist's desk, the driver told her in French that there were guests for the executive suite.

The receptionist nodded. *"Vous pouvez procéder."*

Given the green light, they walked to the elevator at the end of the lobby and stepped in. The driver opened a hidden panel, inside of which was a series of numbered buttons; he pushed the numbers 1-9-9-5. The doors closed in front of them, and the elevator went down. When the doors opened again, they were standing in an underground room full of workers sitting in front of computers.

"General Connors is waiting for you in the office down the hall. Room 6," said the driver before getting back on the elevator.

Simon, Sheila, and Deon walked down the hall to the room, taking in every detail. Many of Twilight's buildings across the globe contained hidden bunkers to be used and accessed by Silhouettes field agents.

"Welcome to Bureau Gamma" said a familiar voice just ahead. Connors stepped outside the meeting room. "After we got the building from the CIA last year we refurbished it and slapped the Twilight Industries logo on it," explained Connors.

"Welcome back, all of you" said Connors.

"It's good to be back, boss," Sheila said warmly.

As they walked into the meeting room Connors stopped Simon. "I see you managed to get the band back together, Simon. " Have to say that I'm impressed," said Connors.

"Let's just get down to business," Simon said as he walked inside. He was glad to be back with the team, but it still bothered him that they'd been split up in the first place.

"By all means, but first, I brought an old friend of ours here," said Connors as they sat down.

Before they could ask who, a young man of Mexican descent with shoulder length black hair walked in. Dressed in a white lab coat, Superman t-shirt, long gray pants, and carrying a large briefcase.

Simon, Sheila and Deon recognized him instantly; the man's name was Eduardo Sanchez, code name: CASH. He served as Silhouette's technology and equipment officer working as Silhouettes liaison to Twilight Industries, overseeing and designing the gadgets and weapons used by their field agents.

"Ed, long time no see!" Deon said warmly.

"Hey, guys!" replied Eduardo, as he joined Connors at the front of the room. They stood in front of a large screen on the wall.

"Seriously, you're still here?" Simon said with an annoyed sigh.

"Great to see you too, Simon" grunted Eduardo icily.

Connors was starting to feel like a teacher in a class full of distracted students. He said, "Ed, you have the floor."

"We've analyzed the data Simon and Deon brought back from San Francisco and we've done a background check on Imran Nadella," Eduardo said, pulling out a remote and aiming it at the large screen behind him.

He walked to the side of the screen so they could see the picture more clearly. A bald man of average height with a short goatee appeared on screen.

"Lady and gentlemen, meet Imran Nadella," Connors said.

"Dude looks like an Arab Heisenberg," Deon said sarcastically.

"Nah, Heisenberg was much shorter than this guy," Simon said.

"You're both wrong, and anyway, Heisenberg wore glasses," said Eduardo.

"Could be wearing contacts," Simon said.

"Five bucks says he doesn't wear either contacts *or* glasses," Deon said slyly.

"You're on," Simon said, slapping his outstretched hand as Sheila rolled her eyes.

Eduardo cleared his throat before speaking. "Intel. says he doesn't wear corrective lenses of any kind. But speaking of things that are actually *important*, he's the head of a multinational shipping company known as Windwaker Transports."

"What about this party of his?" said Simon as he handed a five-dollar bill to Deon.

"Apparently he's holding it to celebrate the launch of his newest and largest cargo ship, the *Hermes.* Some of the richest people in the world will be there – mostly representatives from major corporations like Bloodstone Incorporated, Prometheus Technologies and Wilburscheid and Hammelin, to name a few," explained Eduardo.

"What the hell is Wilburscheid and Hammelin?" Deon asked.

"One of the world's largest law firms," answered Eduardo as he pushed a button on the remote. A picture of an opulent mansion appeared on the screen. "This is where the party is being held: Nadella's mansion in the mountains outside Monte Carlo here in Monaco."

"The rich keep getting richer," Deon muttered dryly.

"What have you found out about these Networc people?" Sheila asked.

"I'll be honest, we still know nothing about the organization," Connors interjected.

"However," Eduardo offered, "Kranz said that Nadella is a major part of the Networc."

"So what's our objective?" Simon asked.

"Your mission is to infiltrate the mansion and try to find out what you can at the party," answered Connors.

Sheila looked at the mansion, which appeared impenetrable.

"What's our insertion plan?" asked Sheila.

"You'll be arriving separately as guests. Your cover is that you're businessmen from Twilight Industries who wish to invest in Windwaker," Connors instructed.

"You'll receive cover IDs later. Once inside the mansion, find out what you can about the Networc," Connors said.

"It's fairly straightforward," chimed in Eduardo.

"Will security be a problem?" Simon asked.

"According to our intel, his security people are ex-military from Applied Dynamics. As for weapons expect small arms like pistols and light SMGs, think ... Uzis and P90s, mostly," answered Connors.

Connors had seen these three in action and knew what they were capable of.

"However," he cautioned, "because of the large civilian presence at the party, we prefer that you limit the use of firearms at all, unless shit happens. And if shit *does* happen, use silencers."

"Wait, how are we gonna get our guns through security?" Deon asked.

"Good question. They won't be frisking guests – bad form, you know. You *should* be fine, but after what happened in 'Frisco they might have metal detectors installed," Connors answered.

"Fortunately, we've managed to circumvent those little nuisances with these," said Eduardo, as he placed his briefcase on the table and opened it. Inside were three watches: a Rolex, a Seiko, and a Timex.

"I love this part," Deon said with a little giggle.

"Yay," said Simon sarcastically.

"Yes, well in*side* each of the watches is a small jamming device that will shield your guns and ammo from any metal detectors as long as you're wearing the watch," replied Eduardo.

Simon picked up the Rolex and looked at it. "How very double-O-7 of you. Is it going to *work* this time?" Simon asked sardonically as he put it on.

"Just because you have had bad luck with my gadgets doesn't mean they don't work," Eduardo frowned.

"Bad luck? Is that what you're calling it?" Simon said.

"It will work," said Eduardo firmly.

"First time for everything," muttered Simon, moving his wrist back and forth studying the watch.

Sheila chose the Seiko, as it had a more feminine style. Deon took the Timex.

"This is all very good but if things go south in there, how are we supposed to get out?" Sheila asked.

"What makes you think they'll go south?" Simon asked.

Sheila glared at Simon, exasperated. "They have before. Remember what happened in Tokyo, One Eye?" she asked.

Simon shrugged, remembering the mission. "As I recall, that mission was a success," he answered drily.

"Then we have very different definitions of success," Sheila replied.

"If you're both done?" interrupted Connors.

Deon coughed lightly. "That's a big 'if,' sir."

Connors blew out a breath. "To answer your question, Sheila, if things 'go south' you have two ex-filtration options: the helicopter out back, or you can fight your way to the parking lot."

"Ride or fly," Deon said.

"Pretty much," nodded Connors.

"We can have the cars return here via remote control," explained Eduardo.

"Self-Driving cars … I like it!" Deon answered, impressed.

"And no one's going to notice three cars driving to the same place by themselves?" asked Simon skeptically.

"The windows are tinted so that no one can see inside yet you can see out. Incidentally, they'll be going to three separate locations in the city where agents will pick the cars up," Eduardo continued.

"Cool," Deon.

"Glad, someone respects my work," Eduardo said glaring at Simon.

"Hey, I respect your work…when it works," said Simon.

Ignoring his sarcasm, Eduardo resumed speaking.

"If you *do* have to make a scene at the party and pistols aren't enough, I have some heavy artillery for you." Reaching into the briefcase, he withdrew three stacks of change, and placed them carefully on the table.

"These look like everyday coins but in reality, they're grenades," explained Eduardo.

"Let's hope they don't blow up in our faces," Simon said drily. Beside him, Sheila rolled her eyes.

"Actually, they're supposed to blow up in the *enemies'* faces, genius" replied Eduardo.

"To trigger them, just press the sides. Once they're triggered, just throw them and BOOM!" said Eduardo excitedly. He gestured for them to take some.

They each complied, studying them.

"Interesting. They look just like euros," Sheila said.

"They're supposed to," said Eduardo, pleased with his handiwork. "By the way, Simon considering your ... um ..." Eduardo struggled nervously for the right words.

"What?" Simon demanded, knowing where this was headed. He'd heard it all before, many times over.

"Optical ... deficiency?"

"Is that what you're calling it now?" Simon asked. "Just come right out and say it. My right eye is an issue, isn't it?"

"Specifically, your lack of one," quipped Deon. Simon shot him a glare.

"Which is why I brought the Janusum," said Eduardo, pulling a stainless steel cigarette case out of his pocket. He tossed it lightly at Simon, who caught it.

Well, here's a walk down memory lane. Janusum was a flesh-colored, putty-like substance that could be rubbed on someone's face and molded to resemble anyone else's. It was usually given to field agents for undercover work and stored in everyday items – a glasses case, a cigarette case. The Janusum kit also came with a pair of fake eyes and hair that would stick to the putty.

The kit was an invaluable tool; all Silhouette agents were trained extensively in its use. In Simon's case, the Janusum would cover up his patch, making him less recognizable. Inside the case was a row of cigarettes concealing a false bottom. that contained the Janusum kit. Simon opened the case and pressed a small hidden switch on the side; the cigarettes flipped up revealing the Janusum and fake eyes and fake mustaches.

"Does it still itch?" Simon asked casually.

"Seriously? That's the first thing you say?" Deon said as Simon closed the case.

"What? It's annoying," Simon said.

Eduardo shrugged as Simon slid the case into his pocket. "Deal with it," grunted Connors.

"Aye, aye, General, sir," Simon said with mock seriousness, giving Connors a sloppy salute.

The general ignored him. It wasn't that discipline was lax; he simply understood the dangers they were voluntarily facing.

"That just about covers it, I think," Connors said. He snapped his fingers. "Oh, before I forget, the party is formal dress only. You'll find your clothing and cover identities upstairs in your rooms." He checked his watch. "Start getting ready. The party's tonight at 1900 hours – that's 7pm, Simon." He grinned.

"No shit" grunted Simon.

"Good luck," he said. He and Eduardo nodded to the group and left the room.

"Just like old times," Deon said dryly.

Chapter 9
Out of the frying pan

They had each been assigned a car to drive to the party. Simon had an Aston Martin DB11; Deon, a Chevrolet V-6LE Camaro. Sheila drove a Mercedes CLA25. One of the perks of being a spy was getting to drive cars that you could never afford otherwise, mused Simon as he drove.

The Janusum on his face made him look like an entirely different person. On top of his eye patch was now a fake eye the same color as his left eye. He wore a black blazer, white dress shirt, black bow tie, and black pants. He glanced up at the rear view mirror.

Simon's Jericho 941 had been fitted with a silencer and was resting in his shoulder holster under his tuxedo jacket. By the time he arrived at the party, Deon was already there. He was drinking champagne by the door in the same style of tuxedo as Simons. Simon walked over to him, weaving his way through groups of elegantly attired men and women talking and drinking. He ignored the drinks as much as possible – the mere sight of them made him feel queasy.

"How's the cream holding up?" Deon asked sarcastically. "Cream" was the nickname agents used for Janusum.

"Itchy as hell," Simon said as a waiter walked past him carrying a tray with three champagne flutes.

For a split second, Simon thought about grabbing one, but he brushed the thought aside.

"How are you holding up?" Deon asked.

"I'm fine," Simon said sternly and quickly, appreciating Deon's concern.

"Is LITHIUM here yet?" asked Simon changing the subject.

"See for yourself," Deon said, gesturing for Simon to turn around.

Sheila had just arrived wearing a red dress with a brilliant gold necklace. As she walked slowly but purposefully toward them, there wasn't a man in the room who could take his eyes off of her.

"Damn," mumbled Simon.

"Lucky bastard," muttered Deon, saluting Sheila with his champagne as she sauntered over to them.

A server offered her champagne, which she politely declined. "Hell of a dress hon," Simon said.

"Thank you, kind sirs. I count three bodyguards so far. What about you?" Sheila asked.

Simon and Deon grinned slightly. "I've got five," answered Deon.

"Just four for me," Simon replied.

"So what now?" Deon asked.

Just then, one of the servers walked to the center of the room to make an announcement. "Ladies and gentlemen, Mr. Nadella would like to see you all in the main hall," he said.

Everyone began moving in the same direction, chatting along the way.

"That answer your question?" Simon asked.

"One of them, anyway," replied Deon.

The three of them followed the others into the main hall. Simon placed his hand over his ear communicator. Silhouette didn't need to monitor *everything*.

"Have I mentioned how stunning you look in that dress?" Simon said.

"One time too many," answered Sheila.

The three of them split up so they wouldn't draw attention and went to different parts of the room.

In another room, Nadella was straightening his tie when one of his guards walked up to him.

"Sir, we've got a problem," said the guard.

"Can it wait? I'm about to address the crowd," replied Nadella.

"I'm afraid not, sir. You should see these," said the guard as he handed him photos of Simon, Deon, and Sheila entering the mansion.

Nadella studied the prints as the guard continued, "The two men kidnapped Kranz and the woman is the writer from Seattle."

"Didn't one of them have an eye patch?" asked Nadella.

"We believe he's wearing some kind of mask," replied the guard.

"Watch them closely," Nadella said.

"Yes sir," the guard replied.

A platform with a podium had been set up at the front of the main hall. Nadella walked into the room and stood at the podium. His guests applauded and then quieted as he began his speech.

Ignoring Nadella's speech, Simon walked over to Sheila.

"Now is a good chance to slip away and investigate while that windbag is talking," whispered Simon. Sheila nodded in agreement.

Simon called Deon on his communicator. "ROUNDABOUT, this is MONOLITH. We're heading in, keep watch."

"You got it," replied Deon from the other side of the room.

Simon and Sheila walked found a door at the back of the room. When no one was looking, they slipped out and found themselves in a hallway.

"Any ideas?" Simon asked.

"If there's anything about the Networc here, it'll be in the server room," Sheila said.

Simon nodded in agreement.

Suddenly they heard a door open at the end of the hall. "Shit, guards," whispered Simon.

An idea occurred to Sheila. She wrapped her arms around Simon and kissed him on the lips. The guards assumed they were just two more drunk, horny party guests. Not the first time.

Once the guards were gone, Sheila let go. "Sorry," Sheila said.

"Don't be," Simon said slyly.

Sheila made a face at him and rolled her eyes. "The guards came from over there," Sheila said, pointing.

They walked briskly to the door and were rather surprised to find it unlocked. They opened it carefully, found it unattended, and went inside. Several huge cabinet-shaped servers dominated the room. In the middle of the room was a small table with a laptop on it, and a chair next to it.

"Jackpot," Simon whistled through his teeth. "Hon, you get what you can while I stand guard." He pulled out his suppressed Jericho and stood by the door, watching the hallway.

Sheila sat down at the table. She pulled a USB drive out of her pocket, placed it in the computer, and began typing.

Deon's whisper in his earpiece informed Simon that Nadella was ending his speech. Simon looked at Sheila nervously. "Are you done yet?" he asked.

"Got it!" Sheila said excitedly as she ejected the drive from the computer. Suddenly an alarm went off and the room was bathed in a flashing red light.

"Shit" grunted Simon.

Simon peered out into the hallway; four guards were headed straight towards them.

"Damn, there's four of them, hon! Odds aren't looking good," he said. Reaching into his pocket, he pulled out one of Eduardo's coins. He squeezed the edges of the coin and threw it at the guards. The explosion propelled them against the wall.

"Huh," Simon said, pleasantly surprised. "It actually worked."

"So I guess there really is a first time for everything," replied Sheila.

She stood close to him now, her silenced P99 poised for action.

The remaining guards positioned themselves outside the room with their Glocks drawn and aimed at the door. Suddenly, Simon and Sheila kicked open the door. Simon killed two of them and Sheila got the other two. Sheila also shot the security camera that was hanging from the roof. Breathing heavily, they looked at each other and smiled.

"Just like old times," Simon said.

"Better," Sheila said.

From down the hall they heard someone yelling, "Get them!"

Two more guards ran towards them and then suddenly, they fell to the ground. Standing over their lifeless bodies, holding a silenced pistol, was Deon.

"I can't leave you two alone for five minutes, can I?" he joked grimly.

"They started it," Simon replied.

"What's the plan?" Deon asked, as he ran to join them.

Simon and Sheila looked at each other, then back at Deon.

"Helicopter," they said together.

"Great, how do we get there?" Deon asked.

Simon walked to the window at the end of the hall and shattered the glass with his gun. "Through here," said Simon.

They climbed out the window one by one and waited until they were all through it.

Once they were all outside, they ran across a courtyard towards the helipad. Suddenly they heard the unmistakable sound of machine gun fire behind them and ducked behind a fountain. From that vantage point, they could see the shooters.

Simon fired back at them with his Jericho hitting two of the shooters.

"ROUNDABOUT! Get the chopper started, we'll cover you!" he yelled.

Deon ran to the chopper, got in, and started the engine while Simon and Sheila covered him with their pistols. As the blades started spinning, Sheila ran to the chopper with Simon providing cover fire. When it was his turn to run, one of Nadella's guards tackled him.

The men wrestled on the ground, but Simon slipped out of the man's grasp and got to his feet, however, not before the guard struck Simon on the right side of the face, dislodging the Janusum mask. Simon backhanded the guard, punched him in the stomach, and delivered a final uppercut, which knocked the guard on his back, unconscious.

Simon ripped off the rest of the Janusum and tossed it aside. He picked up his gun and holstered it when he noticed the fallen guard's Sig 552 submachine gun. Simon picked it up just as several more guards arrived and started shooting at him. Simon cocked the Sig and fired at the guards. As he ran to the chopper and jumped in, he looked back to the three more he'd hit.

"He's in! Get us the hell out of here!" yelled Sheila.

"Yes ma'am," Deon said.

As the helicopter began to rise, Simon and Sheila continued shooting. Once they were out of range of the guns, they stopped and looked at each other. They could feel it between them again, a connection reestablished. They lowered their guns and held hands like two teenagers on their first date as they looked at each other, neither feeling the need to speak.

"You two okay?" Deon called from the cockpit.

"Better than okay," Simon yelled. He and Sheila looked at each other as the helicopter flew through the night to safety.

*****

Nadella watched the helicopter melt into the darkness. "Dammit," he muttered.

"Certainly fucked this up, didn't you?" said a voice behind him.

Nadella turned around and was surprised to see the Networc agent, Counselor Black, standing behind him.

"I saw you at the party. What are you doing here?" Nadella tried not to sound nervous.

Counselor Black casually walked up to him, his hands in his trench coat pockets, his eyes surveying the damage.

"From what I saw, three professionals stole sensitive intel. regarding Project: Big Picture from you and also took out a good portion of your security force. What do you have to say for yourself?" Counselor Black asked.

"Look I have no...heeeey! Wait a minute. What are you even doing here?" Nadella demanded. There was no reason for a member of the Networc's Upper Echelon to be at his mansion.

As a member of the Networcs controlling organ known as the Board of Directors, Nadella knew that its men like Black, referred to as Counselors, belonged to a branch of the Networc called the Upper Echelon, which specialized in covert operations – specifically, assassinations. As he pondered this fact, another fact came right on its heels: He had not been notified by the board that Black was coming.

Counselor Black looked to his left and right, counting the dead guards, kicking a few of the bullet casings strewn across the heliport. He smiled and shifted his gaze back to Nadella.

"The Board of Directors had concerns about your security and sent me to investigate," he said.

"Why?" Nadella asked.

"Really?" Counselor Black snapped.

"You really have to ask 'why'? Let's hope your successor is better at keeping secrets than you have been." In a single movement, Black pulled out a silenced Glock 17 and shot Nadella in the head.

Counselor Black turned around and looked at the remaining two guards, injured but ambulatory.

"Let's go," he told them.

The guards stood up and followed Counselor Black to his car. Once inside, Counselor Black pulled out his cellphone, dialed a familiar number and waited until he heard the scrambled voice of the Networc's leader.

"Hello," Mr. Zero said.

"Mr. Zero, all loose ends have been neutralized," Counselor Black reported.

"What about the attackers and the compromised files?" asked Mr. Zero.

"Unfortunately, they got away with the files, but by the time those interlopers realize the scale of Operation: Big Picture, it'll be too late," Black answered, hoping his response appeased the man.

"Very well, keep me in the loop," Mr. Zero said before hanging up.

"Yes sir," replied Counselor Black.

Meanwhile, thousands of miles away in Switzerland in the opulent office on the top floor of the skyscraper-headquarters of Kronos International, Counselor Black's superior, the enigmatic leader of the Networc – a man referred to by his underlings only as Mr. Zero – sat calmly at his desk. He put the phone down and looked at his computer screen. A window containing a satellite photo of a Belarusian military bunker appeared there, with the words Sankcyja Sini.

Mr. Zero leaned back in his chair and smiled with confidence. "The game is afoot," he said to himself.

Chapter 10
...And into the Fire

Simon was the first to awaken. The morning sun was shining into the room. Scattered haphazardly around the room were two sets of clothes from the night before. He turned over just as Sheila's eyes were starting to open. He looked at her warmly as the sun shone on her face.

"Sleep well?" Simon asked cheekily.

"You know I didn't," Sheila said with a knowing grin, placing her hand on Simon's naked chest.

Their eyes met and it was as if all that had ever existed was them and all that had ever been was this moment. Gone was the anger, the doubt. All that was left was love.

"So much for taking it slow," Simon said a little groggily.

Sheila laughed coquettishly. "We've never been the slow and steady type."

"We're more *Fast and Furious*," Simon said dryly as he got out of the bed and put on his bathrobe. "Deon said that about your book – *James Bond* meets the *Fast and Furious*."

Sheila sat up in bed, her naked alluring body barely covered by the blankets. "I toned down the love scenes, don't worry. Hey! Where are you going?" Sheila asked, stretching.

"Balcony," answered Simon. "But first ..." He put his knee on the bed and kissed her passionately on her luscious red lips. He broke away, opened the sliding door, and walked out on the balcony.

From the balcony of his room at Twilight Industries, Simon could see almost all of Monaco. Sheila slipped on her robe, walked up to Simon, and embraced him from behind, placing her hands on his chest and resting her head on his back. Simon placed his hand on hers as they stood there holding each other quietly.

"I think we broke the bed," joked Sheila in a loud whisper.

"We'll send Connors a bill," muttered Simon.

Sheila let go of him and walked to his side, resting her hands on the balcony rail.

"So about last night. What does it mean for our … future – or am I reading too much into it?" Simon asked.

Sheila shrugged, "I don't know if last night was adrenaline, passion, or both," answered Sheila as she turned to embrace him again. "But I do know that 'whatever will be will be,'" Sheila sang lightly.

"Que sera sera," Simon replied, as their lips grew closer to each other.

"Show off," said Sheila as their lips met and they held each other in their arms.

*****

At that very moment, in the luxury hotel across the street, two agents of the Networc's Upper Echelon were watching and listening. These particular Networc agents usually had orders to obtain footage to be used for blackmailing politicians and celebrities. Ordinarily, they would have ignored the footage of a couple enjoying the morning sun and each other. However, late last night they and every other Networc agent in the area received orders from Counselor Black to keep an eye out for the three agents that attacked Nadella's party and to notify him immediately if they spotted them. He'd sent all agents photographs of the attackers taken with hidden cameras at the mansion.

The agents instantly recognized the two lovers in the footage as two of the three. Confirming their identities, they followed Counselor Black's orders to the letter.

Ten minutes Counselor Black was looking at the clouds below his private plane when his cell phone rang.

"Who is this?" asked Black.

The two agents identified themselves as Counselors Cancro and Stetson, respectively. The two Networc agents told him about their discovery. Counselor Black thanked them and hung up.

Clearly, these people were professionals of extraordinary skill, requiring extraordinary, immediate methods to be dealt with. He dialed the number of a Lower Echelon Unit in Monaco and ordered them to follow both

Simon and Sheila, killing them on sight should they leave the building.

Normally he would do it himself but this seemed more like a job for the Networc's commandos, referred to as the Lower Echelon. It was not only because of their skills; killing them in public, in broad daylight, would either discourage whomever they were working for from investigating further, or at least slow them down considerably.

*****

Sheila took a shower while Simon watched the news on television. The main story was the continued escalation of the Belarusian civil war. He hadn't used his knowledge of French in several years, but he found it all coming back. He was barely paying attention as the anchor talked about how the United Nations was planning on sending mediators to the embattled nation.

Suddenly there was a knock at the door. Simon got up, looked through the peephole, and opened the door.

"Hey, Deon what's up?" Simon asked.

"Just letting you know that Connors and Ed are going to be going through those files you and Sheila got last night," Deon said. "Speaking of Sheila – have you seen her? She wasn't in her room just now."

In answer to his question, Sheila yelled from behind the bathroom's flimsy door. "Morning, Deon!"

"Wait, if she's ... oh my god! Simon. You didn't!" Deon said, surprised. Simon just grinned silently in answer.

"You *did*, didn't you?" replied Deon.

"Bye, Deon," Simon said as he pushed closed the door.

Simon could hear Deon laughing as he walked down the hall to the elevator. Sheila walked out of the bathroom wearing nothing but a towel.

"What did Deon want?" Sheila asked.

"Deon, Connors, and Ed are gonna be downstairs decrypting the data you got off that drive," answered Simon.

"Great, so what the hell are we supposed to do all day?" Sheila asked.

"We could ...," Simon said, grinning suggestively.

"We've already done that," Sheila replied bluntly. "A few times."

"Then, I have another idea," Simon offered.

"I'll just bet you do," Sheila said as she rolled her eyes. "Go on," said Sheila.

Simon sat down on the little sofa in front of the television and patted the place beside him. Sheila joined him.

"The last time we had any real fun together was our last wedding anniversary. Why don't we go out and enjoy ourselves while we're here on the French Riviera? Hell, it sure beats sitting here watching TV," suggested Simon.

Sheila was delighted by the idea. "You know what? Fuck it. Let's do it!" she replied.

"Great, I'll call Connors and tell him," Simon said, reaching for his phone.

"And I'll get dressed," replied Sheila as she stood up.

"Take your time," Simon said quietly.

Sheila glared at him before laughing softly. "You always were good at making me laugh," said Sheila as she got her clothes out.

Watching her, Simon grinned as he picked up the phone, punched in the number for the bunker, and told Connors their plan. After some convincing, he agreed. "It's a go, hon," Simon said. "The old coot even said 'have fun' before he hung up."

"Well, get dressed," Sheila said.

A quick dresser from years on the run, she was already dressed in white pants, a black leather jacket, and a black T-shirt.

"What about that red dress?" Simon asked.

"You know I hate dressing up. Why don't *you* wear it?" she joked.

"Very funny," Simon said, frowning. "You know red isn't my color."

As Simon got dressed, Sheila shut off the TV.

"Ready when you are, hon," Simon said. He was dressed in his usual clothes: dark green pants, black shirt, and dark blue trench coat.

"Seriously though, after all these years you *still* wear that ugly ass trench coat?" Sheila asked mockingly.

"And you still have that ugly ass black jacket?" Simon asked jokingly.

"It's called style," she retorted.

Sheila walked across the room casually with Simon following behind her.

They rode the elevator down to the lobby, talking about what they planned for the day. A convertible was waiting for them downstairs, courtesy of Twilight Industries.

"I'll drive," Simon said, unaware that they were being watched.

They decided to drive back to Nice. It was a beautiful day as people went about their daily routines under the warm sun. Having a day to themselves while on a mission was a rarity for people in there line of work so whenever they got the opportunity they seized it.

As they drove along the road, Simon cast frequent glances at Sheila, enjoying the way her hair blew in the wind. When she caught his eye, she smiled back.

In Nice, Simon parked in front of a row of stores that faced the beach. They walked hand in hand down an alley leading to a small outdoor café with a courtyard.

Unseen, but watching them surreptitiously from the rooftops, was a spotter for a Networc assassin. He was armed with an M40A5 sniper rifle. "Targets have arrived. Proceeding with assassination, sir," radioed the spotter. The sniper reached into his pocket, pulled out a black suppressor, and screwed it onto the barrel of the rifle.

Even when they were married, people looked at them strangely when they went out in public. A beautiful, blonde like Sheila with Simon, an otherwise-attractive man with an eye patch raised eyebrows. The stares and whispers about them never bothered either of them as they just ignored it; today in Nice, it was no different. Simon and Sheila sat down at a table and ordered coffee and croissants in fluent French. After a few minutes, the waiter returned with their orders.

"So … once this is all over, where do we go from here?" Simon asked as he took a gulp of coffee.

"Maybe we could just … wing it and see what happens," Sheila said, shrugging before taking a bite out of a croissant.

"Works for me," replied Simon, feeling relieved as he took another drink of coffee. He was relieved by her answer.

"So how's the life of a bestselling author treating you?" asked Simon.

"Honestly, it's boring as hell, endless meetings with editors and publicists. What about you?" Sheila asked.

"Pretty much the same. Boring. I just do security consultation work. Although I *was* hired to be a military consultant on some movie last year with that guy from the Matrix, Reeves something-or-other," Simon teased.

"Keanu Reeves?" Sheila asked.

Simon snapped his fingers in mock realization. "Yeah, that's the guy," replied Simon.

"What's he like?" asked Sheila.

"He's really into the fight choreography, he was always asking me to show him stuff" answered Simon.

"Huh, I always thought he was one of those fake tough guys," replied Sheila sounding mildly surprised.

"The hell is a fake tough guy?" asked Simon.

"You know, guys like Liam Neeson they act tough but really anyone could kick there ass" clarified Sheila.

"How is Liam Neeson a fake tough guy?" asked Simon.

"Come on, there is no way that some old Irish guy really does all those stunts" said Sheila.

"You just don't like Liam Neeson" Simon replied.

"And? Those Taken movies are bullshit!" said Sheila.

Simon rolled his eyes, "Hollywood, hon" replied Simon with a shrug.

Suddenly, two men walked up behind Sheila, one of them put his hand on her shoulder.

"Mademoiselle, a beautiful woman like you would be much happier with us," said the man in perfect English.

Instinctively, Simon and Sheila studied them, sized them up. Despite their muscular frames, Simon and Sheila could easily deal with them if they had to.

"Listen fellas, we're just trying to enjoy ourselves," Simon said.

The other man looked at Simon and pushed him out of the chair with his hand, laughing rudely.

"Now then, how about you spend your day with some real men?" said the man with his hand on Sheila.

Simon looked up at Sheila from the cobblestone sidewalk and grinned. She grinned back, understanding perfectly.

Sheila looked back up at the man and batted her eyelashes primly. "Sure, do you know any?" answered Sheila sarcastically. In the next split second, she grabbed his hand and pulled it off her shoulder, suddenly she slammed her foot down on his causing him to fall to his knees in pain. Sheila then backhanded him with one hand, knocking him out.

As soon as she moved, Simon grabbed his coffee cup, jumped to his feet, and slammed the cup into the other man's face, shattering the cup. Before he could respond, Simon kicked the other man in the stomach knocking him to the ground.

The other diners were aghast. Simon looked over at them and casually held up his coffee cup. "Check please," he said with a wry smile.

One of the waiters ran over and told them to leave before he called the police. Simon and Sheila shrugged and paid for their food, deciding it wasn't worth having to call Connors to bail them out. They bowed slightly to the waiter and patrons, and walked away from the café.

"Just like in Hong Kong," Sheila said as they walked down the narrow street.

"The only difference is that there were four of them that time," said Simon.

Sheila shook her head. "Details, details," she said.

Simon suddenly shoved her behind a dumpster and jumped behind it with her.

"What the hell?" yelled Sheila.

Simon pointed to the building across the street from the coffee shop. In the bright sunlight, the glare of the sniper's rifle on the roof was impossible to miss to a trained eye.

"Shit!" Sheila said as the sniper fired two rounds, barely missing them.

"Head for the car!" yelled Simon as he pulled out his Jericho 941; he fired three rounds at the sniper to give her cover.

Sheila had her P99 drawn as well. She ran to the car wondering if she was going to lose Simon just as she was starting to fall in love with him again.

As she approached the car, she heard the unmistakable sound of machine-gun fire and ducked behind the car. Looking up, she saw a white van speeding towards her with a man in the passenger seat firing a machine gun at her. Sheila aimed her P99 at the car and fired two shots. One of the bullets hit the driver, while the other hit the gunman. The van swerved out of control and crashed into a light post on the other side of the street. Sheila smiled, pleased she hadn't lost her shooting skills. Suddenly four men jumped out of the back of the van.

"Oh, shit," Sheila said, ducking behind the car again.

As the gunmen opened fire, she fired back, hitting one square in the chest. Simon fired a fourth and final round at the sniper. The man fell from the roof, crashing onto a café table below. Hearing the gunshots in the street, Simon ran out to help Sheila, finding a vantage spot around a building not far from her.

"The service here is terrible, hon!" yelled Simon.

Sheila was relieved he was alive. "Yeah! Remind me to complain to the manager," she called. "What about the sniper?"

"What sniper?" answered Simon. He leaned out from cover and fired just two rounds at the gunmen before hearing the telltale *click-click*. "Fuck! I'm out of ammo!" he yelled as he quickly reloaded.

"Cover me, I'm headed for the car," yelled Sheila.

As soon as his gun was reloaded, Simon fired while Sheila ran to the car, jumped inside, and got it started. With the convertible top down, she was an easy mark for the gunman aiming at her head, but Simon fired three shots at him, killing him.

As the car roared to life, she backed up to where Simon was standing. "Sometime today, One Eye!" she barked.

"Whatever you say, hon," Simon replied as he dove into the car.

Once he was inside, Sheila swung it around so that it faced the assassin's car. With a loud screech, she barreled toward the assassins, running over one of them.

"Should have looked both ways," Simon shouted.

Before Sheila could respond, a barrage of bullets hit the back of the car.

Simon turned around. A pickup truck with an M249 SAW heavy machine gun in the back was closing in.

"Uh, hon, there's a SAW behind us," Simon said with more calmness than he felt.

"Of course there is," Sheila replied. "'Let's go to the Riviera!' he said. ' We'll have fun!' he said," complained Sheila.

"Seemed like a good idea at the time," replied Simon sardonically.

Simon fired at the truck's driver but to no avail. "Fuck! The damn thing has bullet proof windows," he yelled.

Sheila saw that they were approaching a turn that overlooked the harbor, which gave her an idea.

"Hold on!" Sheila yelled.

As they approached the fence, Sheila made a hard left turn then kept going narrowly avoiding a collision with the concrete guardrail. The truck approached the turn couldn't maneuver as quickly; crashing through the wall, it landed on a boat in the harbor.

"I guess they decided to go fishing instead," Sheila said sardonically.

"Really?" replied Simon. He let his head fall back on the seat.

"Piss off; I thought it was funny," grunted Sheila.

"I'm glad someone did," said Simon.

When they returned to Twilight Industries, they parked in the back and headed straight for the bunker to tell Connors what happened. They found Connors, Eduardo, and Deon sitting at a computer console in the control room.

"You would not believe the traffic on the way here," said Simon.

"We were monitoring what was going on via police band and satellite," said Connors.

"Trouble just seems to find us," replied Sheila sarcastically.

"The guys that attacked us were either from the Networc or they were Nadella's goons," said Simon.

"Not Nadella. He was found dead this morning," said Connors.

"Which only leaves the Networc," added Deon.

"Makes sense. The intel. we've been able to get out of that drive so far is pretty detailed," Eduardo said.

"Speaking of the drive ...," said Sheila, her eyebrows raised in anticipation.

"I'm glad you asked. General, the floor is yours," invited Eduardo.

"The data was heavily encrypted," said Connors. "We could only decrypt some of it, but we did find out that the Networc contacted a Russian official we all know: Yuri Menshov."

Simon whistled. They were all surprised by the connection, but Simon most of all.

"I thought he was dead," said Deon.

"He's lucky he isn't" Connors replied.

"Where is he?" Simon asked.

"He lives in a penthouse in Moscow," answered Connors.

"I'll go talk to him," Simon volunteered.

"Hold on, Simon." Sheila tapped his arm. "Connors, if Menshov is involved does that mean that Red Curtain's involved too?"

Connors had known them all long enough to know when they were nervous. Of the numerous shadow agencies, Silhouette considered enemies, few were as cunning and brutal as Silhouette's Russian equivalent AKA Red Curtain.

"Don't worry about Menshov. He's no longer with Red Curtain. After he tried to kill Simon, he was discharged," reassured Connors.

"But there's something else you all need to know. Soon after you two left this morning, we intercepted a phone call to several people in Monaco. They were no doubt the assassins who tried to kill you. So we are obviously getting to them," continued Connors.

"Because of that, Simon, I'm sending Deon with you to Moscow," said Connors.

"Fine," Simon replied.

"And what about me?" Sheila asked.

Connors picked up a pen and studied it. "Among the intel. we could get from the drive was a list that contained the names of several organizations affiliated with the Networc. The most prominent is a radical ultra-nationalist terrorist organization in Nicaragua known as the New People's Army – NPA for short," said Connors.

He looked at Sheila. "You're going to Nicaragua to investigate their connection to the Networc. Once there, you'll rendezvous with two CIA agents," Connors continued.

"Great, reminds me of the old days," Sheila said sarcastically. She wasn't surprised she was given the Nicaragua assignment, given she had been a member of the CIA's Special Activities Division prior to joining Silhouette.

"When do we leave?" Simon asked.

"No time like the present. The full story is in a dossier on the plane," Connors said.

Chapter 11
The Past Never Forgets

Simon and Deon had been to Russia a handful of times before, few of them pleasant. It was dark by the time they landed at Sheremetyevo Airport in Moscow. A Twilight Industries agent waited with a car and the address for Menshov's penthouse. The men shook hands all around; Deon got behind the wheel and Simon slid in next to him.

"So why exactly does Menshov hate you?" Deon asked, as he drove.

Simon was initially confused at his question until he remembered that Deon wasn't on that mission.

"Years ago I killed his son," answered Simon, he sighed not proud of his answer.

Deon grimaced. "Mind explaining why?" Deon had been with Simon on so many missions, it always surprised him to learn about one on which he hadn't.

Simon shrugged his shoulders. "I don't mind, it's ancient history. Connors had a lead on a Chechen terrorist cell based out of an apartment in Berlin. He sent Sheila and me to 'talk' to them. There were three of them in the apartment," Simon said, replaying it again in his mind.

"I went in first and Sheila followed. We ended up killing two of them. However, one of the two was foreign intelligence, an undercover SVR agent who also happened to be Menshov's son. Once he found out, he swore that he would avenge his son's death by killing me," continued Simon.

"Well, hot damn, aren't you a popular guy?" Deon asked sarcastically.

"Yeah, tell me about it," replied Simon replied drily.

"According to Connors, Menshov is no longer part of Red Curtain," Deon reasoned, "so we don't have to worry about them, right?"

"He's actually the lucky one," Simon replied.

"What did he do that got him kicked out anyway?" asked Deon curiously.

"He used Red Curtain funds and assets to hire guild assassins to try and kill me. Several Red Curtain agents were killed in the process," Simon explained. "As a result they fired him. He should have been killed for that. *Ergo* – lucky," continued Simon.

Deon peered at the street signs. "The dossier mentioned something about him having ties to the Vasilev Syndicate. Do you think that's bullshit?"

"He probably does. He was one of the most powerful men in Russia, but now he's just a broken, angry old man," Simon said as the car slowed to a stop outside a large ornate hotel.

Simon pulled on a pair of black gloves before checking and holstering his Jericho 941. "Stay in the car. I'll handle this," said Simon.

Deon grunted softly as Simon got out of the car and entered the hotel. He walked across the lobby filled with wealthy Russian *nomenklatura* and entered the elevator, pushing the correct button. The elevator went straight to the penthouse. Simon had his weapon ready to face what was on the other side of the doors, but when they opened, it was to an empty space that reeked of wealth and power.

Simon walked over to the kitchen and opened the refrigerator. A bottle of vodka stared right at him, tempting him. He looked away and instead, helped himself to a sandwich made from various foods he found. Rifling through the drawers under the counter he found a small CZ 75 automatic pistol. He picked it up and removed the magazine.

In the middle of the living room was an armchair that faced the elevator. In front of it was a small coffee table. Simon turned off the lights, put Menshov's gun on the coffee table, sat down in the armchair, and began eating. A half hour later, when Menshov returned, he walked inside and turned on the lights instinctively.

"Thanks for the sandwich," Simon said, in perfect Russian.

Menshov turned around, surprised at the sight of his visitor, but he didn't show it. His eyes darted to the gun on the table.

"Don't bother; it's empty," Simon said as he held up the magazine and placed it on the coffee table in front of him.

"Are you here to finish what you started with my son?" asked Menshov as he sat down in a chair in front of Simon.

"That was an accident," Simon said softly.

"The arrogance of you Americans is astounding! You think you can break into my home, eat my food, and tell me that my son's death *by your hand* was an accident?" said Menshov angrily.

Simon sighed. "Look – what happened, happened. And I am sorry but …"

"You say that like it vindicates you. You didn't have to tell my wife and family that our son was taken from us," interrupted Menshov.

"You didn't have to bury him. Don't you dare attempt to apologize for the hell you put my family through, bastard!" Continued Menshov.

"Be that as it may, I'm not here to kill you," Simon said. "In fact, I came to ask for your help."

Menshov burst out laughing, but there was no humor in the sound. "You must be joking. Why would I help the man who took my son from me?" asked Menshov.

Simon leaned forward for emphasis. "Because the lives of potentially millions of sons just like yours is at stake," answered Simon.

"What the hell are you talking about?" barked Menshov.

"Oh, I think you know what I'm talking about," snapped Simon. "The Networc."

At the mention of the Networc, Menshov's face went white with fear, an emotion Simon never expected to see on the face of the former Russian intelligence kingpin. Menshov dropped into a chair and buried his face in his hands. He started to cry, but he quickly pulled back the tears. Simon, stunned at the sight, wondered who these people were that could a reaction in a man like Menshov. He looked up at Simon in anguish.

"I don't know who they are. I don't think anyone does. They sought me out to learn the location of Sankcyja Sini," answered Menshov..

Simon was confused. He had never heard of a town or area named "Sankcyja Sini" before. Maybe his Russian was a little rusty, but he knew enough to know that Sankcyja Sini in English was Sanction Blue.

"Okay, I'll bite," Simon said anxiously. "What the hell is Sanction Blue?" Simon asked.

Menshov relaxed a little as he focused on details. "Several years ago the Belarusian government began developing chemical, biological and nuclear weapons at a Soviet era facility code named Sanction Blue."

"Okay, but where does the Networc come in?" Simon asked.

"I don't know why they want it or how they know of it, but when they found out that I knew of its location, they paid me Twenty million rubles for the information," said Menshov.

"Why?" Simon was shocked by the enormity of Menshov's words.

Menshov was indignant. "How dare you ask 'why' when it's your fault to begin with!?After you killed my son, I was discharged from Red Curtain and left with nothing, just the memory of my now-dead wife and son, and a daughter who won't speak to me. I couldn't transition from *something* to *nothing*," admitted Menshov, ashamed. "So in a moment of weakness, I greedily betrayed the motherland."

Simon jumped to his feet. "Screw the motherland! You've placed the lives of millions at risk!"

"Don't you think I know that, you arrogant bastard? It is just one of the many sins that I will suffer for in hell," Menshov moaned and held out his hands in defeat and penance. "So just kill me and get it over with."

"Kill you?" Simon said, confused.

"Yes, go ahead and kill me. Isn't that what your masters sent you here to do? You've already taken so much from me. Finish what you started with my son and kill me! Send me to my son!" Menshov collapsed in great sobs, waiting for the deathblow.

Simon walked to the elevator and pushed the ground floor button. "I told you already – I wasn't sent here to kill you. If you want to die so badly, do it yourself. I don't kill unarmed men," said Simon sternly.

When the door opened, Simon walked in turned around. Menshov raised his head and they locked eyes. As the doors closed, Simon saw Menshov get up from his chair. As the elevator began its descent, he heard a single gunshot from the penthouse.

"*Dasvidaniya*," Simon said quietly.

Even though he had tried to kill Simon on numerous occasions, Simon respected him, even pitied him. After all, what happened to Menshov could have happened to Simon. But where Menshov stared into the abyss and was consumed by it, Simon fought his way out from its grasp. The elevator doors opened and Simon was once again in a lobby filled with the rich, the powerful, and the visiting – all oblivious to the suicide that had just taken place above them. He shrugged off the introspection and walked outside to the car. He saw Deon reading a book in the driver's seat as he approached it.

"What are you reading?" Simon asked as he got into the car, only half interested.

"Sheila's book, how'd it go?" asked Deon.

"I said my goodbyes," Simon said as Deon put the book aside to start the car.

As they drove to the airport, Deon noticed a car following them in the rear view mirror. Simon saw it in the side mirror. It's windows were tinted black.

"Deon ..." Simon began.

"Yeah, I see it. Think it's Red Curtain?" said Deon.

He responded by speeding up a little.

"I'd rather not find out, if it's all the same to you," Simon replied.

In response the car sped up and moved into the lane next to them, as it began approaching them. Instead, the rear passenger window of the car slid down to reveal a handholding.

"Me neither," Deon said. He pulled a coin grenade out of his pocket, squeezed the edges, and tossed it out the window at the car before pressing the accelerator to the floor.

Behind them, the black car exploded, crashing into a sidewalk bench.

"And you said the traffic in Monaco was bad," replied Deon drily. They continued to the airport without further incident, tacitly concluding that no conversation was needed.

Chapter 12
Rat-a-tat Revolution

After her international flight to Nicaragua, Sheila took a single engine Cessna 172 to a private airport outside of a small coastal mining town known as Castoňa. A CIA agent leaned against the pre-arranged black jeep waiting to pick her up. She stepped out of the plane and approached him.

The agent straightened up and held out his hand. "I'm Foswell. You must be from the SAD?" he said as they shook hands.

"I am," Sheila answered.

"Your reputation precedes you, Agent LITHIUM," Foswell said casually as he got in the car.

"Wonder how that happened?" Sheila said with a wry smile as she got into the front passenger seat.

Foswell was silent as they left the airport and drove down the jungle road that led to the village.

"So what do you know about these NPA guys?" Sheila asked over the jeep's engine.

"Basically they're a group of FARC commandos that split off and went into business for themselves," answered Foswell matter-of-factly.

"I thought FARC's based in Colombia. The 'Revolutionary Armed Forces of Colombia' seems pretty clear on that. What are they doing in Nicaragua?" Sheila asked.

"Good question. Apparently FARC didn't like the idea of having competition, so they chased them out and they settled here," answered Foswell.

Once they pulled into town, they made a left and arrived at a small house with a small garage next to it. They parked outside.

"What are we doing here?" Sheila asked as she looked around the neighborhood. It looked like her old neighborhood in Seattle – peaceful, idyllic, filled with normal everyday people.

"Not what you expected, is it?" Foswell said with a knowing smile. "Welcome to black site 37R where we keep an eye on the NPA."

As he and Sheila stepped out of the car and walked into the garage, Foswell walked to the fuse box on the wall and flipped a switch. A section of wall slid away revealing a set of stairs going down.

"After you, señorita," Foswell said, gesturing to the steps. Sheila grinned and walked downstairs.

Foswell closed the fuse box and followed her. At the bottom of the stairs was a bookshelf, cot, small refrigerator, and rows of computers and miscellaneous equipment.

She noticed, to her surprise, that there was no one else there. "I was told that there would be two of you guys here. Where's your buddy? Corben, right?" Sheila asked.

Foswell crossed his arms. "Two days ago he was sent to infiltrate the NPA base and I haven't heard from him since."

"So where's the base?" Sheila asked.

Foswell seemed surprised by the question. "They're holed up in an abandoned mine in the mountains outside of town. Why do you ask?"

Sheila rolled her eyes. "Because I'm going to go there and rescue him? Duh!" answered Sheila.

"By yourself?" Foswell asked incredulously.

"No, I'm gonna bring Chuck Norris and Sylvester Fucking Stallone with me," she said with a smirk.

She grew more serious. "Now tell me what I'm gonna face up there," asked Sheila.

Foswell sighed. "Okay then, there are around 50 guys up there with basic military training. As for firearms, expect pistols, SMGs and AK-47s," he said.

"Reminds me of a mission in Beirut," Sheila mused.

"All right, I'll leave tomorrow morning. Do you have a map of the compound?"

Foswell nodded and sat down in front of the computer. Soon a satellite map of the compound was on the screen. Foswell pointed to it as he gave his tactical advice. "Basically, your only entrance is through this fence at the base of the mountain. Once you get through the fence, you'll be able to enter the actual mine through this elevator. That's the metal shaft you see here," said Foswell.

"How many are guarding the elevator?" Sheila asked.

Foswell was somber. "Around 12, but don't worry – I can hack their coms and create a distraction," he said.

"Right, Oh and by the way, I'm gonna have to borrow your motorcycle," Sheila said.

"It's chilly in the mines. Bundle up," advised Foswell.

Sheila walked over to a coat rack next to the door and fingered a black leather jacket. "Can I borrow this?"

"Sure. In fact your boy CASH sent it here just for you," replied Foswell. "I was going to give it to you."

"He thought of everything," muttered Sheila as she studied it.

Foswell nodded. "According to his instructions, it's actually a parachute," he said.

"How's it work?" Sheila asked.

Foswell joined her at the coat rack. "According to his instructions, it's pretty simple. See these straps on the inside? Activate the parachute by pulling the top button. There's a beacon hidden in the interior pocket that will broadcast your location to me," he explained.

"A parachute…that should do me a lot of good in a mine," she said with a smile, taking the coat down and putting it on.

"Hey you never know," Foswell, quipped. "Hopefully you won't need to use the 'chute, but it will be nice and warm, anyway."

The next morning Sheila rode to the compound on the agent's dirt bike. It was located at the edge of town at the end of a dirt road overlooking the ocean.

She ditched the bike and hid on the other side of the road, peeking around a large boulder to get her first real look at the place. *Their security is pitiful,* she thought. *That's good for me, though!*

A weathered brick wall with a metal fence as a gate surrounded the compound. Sheila leaned back behind the rock and called Foswell on the communicator in her ear.

"Foswell, whatever you're gonna do, do it now," muttered Sheila.

"Roger. Be advised there's some kind of signal jamming device inside. So once you're in I won't be able to contact you," Foswell replied.

A few minutes later, the gates opened and a large truck carrying twelve guerillas drove out. "How the hell did you do that?" Sheila radioed.

"I sent out a phony distress call saying that their guys in town were in a firefight with government troops."

"Of course you did," she said.

Sheila ran to the brick wall and climbed over it. Once inside, she pulled out her pistol, a silenced Walther P99. She was behind a garage and quickly looked around the edge. After seeing there was no one there she ran to the open elevator on the other side of the compound. When she pushed the Up button, the cage jerked a little bit before rising into the shaft.

A full five minutes passed before the elevator stopped. Sheila now faced the dark interior of the mine. On the ground were tracks for the mine cars. She cocked her gun and slowly walked into the mine. As she approached the first corner, a commando walked in front of her out of nowhere. Before he could aim his rifle at her or even react to her surprise appearance, she'd fired two rounds at his temple, killing him instantly.

Jumping behind the wall, she listened for more commandos and waited, cursing herself for not bringing a suppressor. After about three minutes, she sighed in relief, and looked down at the body of the man she had just killed, taking the time now to look more closely. He was dressed in military fatigues and carried several clips for his AK-47. She hung the gun strap over her shoulder and pocketed the magazines before proceeding down the mineshaft.

As she warily turned the next corner, she passed a mine cart and kept moving. Eventually she ran into a freight elevator. Stepping in, she pushed its Up button. The rose smoothly, but the trip was much shorter than before. It stopped behind a warehouse. Sheila cautiously stepped off and looked out from behind the warehouse. In front of her was a huge courtyard filled with ancient ruins.

In the middle of the ruins was a track that led straight to a mine tunnel. To make matters worse, there were a dozen guards were scattered throughout the ruins. Most were standing by a gas truck on the far left of the compound.

Sheila grinned as an idea began to form in her mind. Holstering her pistol, she cocked the AK – 47, aimed it at the tank of the gas truck, and fired three rounds at the tank.

The tank exploded, sending bodies, fire, and car parts in all directions. Instantly, everyone else ran over to the inferno to try and douse the flames while she ran for the tunnel in the ensuing confusion.

As she entered the tunnel, Sheila looked back at the inferno of her own making. "Huh, actually worked" she muttered.

Walking through the mineshaft, an angry voice yelled above her. She followed the noise down the tunnel, made a left into another tunnel, to a ladder at the end. She climbed up ladder, still following the voice, until – there. She froze, as her eyes were high enough to see.

An NPA leader stood over a table yelling into a cellphone. Another man, blindfolded and tied up, sat beaten in a chair. Sheila finished climbing up the ladder, snuck up behind the leader, and hit him on the head with the butt of her rifle, knocking him out cold. She put his phone in her pocket before running to the man in the chair.

Removing his blindfold she whispered, "Corben, right?"

Corben was barely alive. He gasped, "Yes. Philippines. Kill Counselor Black. Must."

"Who's Counselor Black?" Sheila asked anxiously.

"Networc agent in charge of Big Picture. If project succeeds …," said Corben just as he breathed his last.

A slight noise behind her made her turn. The leader had a gun aimed right at her. "His death is the first of many, bitch," the leader said in English.

In response, Sheila aimed her AK at him. "Drop the gun, asshole," she ordered.

A strange smile crossed the man's face. "So you can beat the truth out of me? No," the man said chillingly. "I think I'll die a little sooner than the rest of us." He placed the muzzle of the pistol under his chin. "Death to America" he muttered.

The leader pulled the trigger and fell over dead before Sheila could react. She walked over to the body and spit on it. "You wish."

There was nothing else in the way of evidence or intel. she could gather there. She climbed down the ladder, walked down a hallway. Hearing something, she hid behind a corner, leaning out and instantly back. Five guerrilla commandos were heading her way.

Sheila took a deep breath, leaned out of cover, aimed, and fired a short burst that killed three of the guerrillas before she leaned back into cover. The other two jumped behind a mine cart and returned fire. Sheila leaned out again and fired, killing both. But more were coming. She ran down the tunnel. *Fuck.* The tunnel ended outside facing a cliff.

"End of the line, bitch," one of the men said. Seven guerrillas stood between her and the tunnel, ready for the kill.

Outnumbered and outgunned, Sheila shuddered at the thought of what these bastards would do to her – either kill her or sell her to the Rojas Cartel, where she would end up as a sex slave or worse. Either way she was screwed. And just that quickly, her years of training kicked in. *There's got to be a way out of this.*

It came to her like something out of an action movie. She tossed her machine gun on the ground and smiled devilishly, eyes locked onto a grenade she spotted on one of the men's belt.

"Smiling in the face of death? Admirable, but futile. Any last words, American?" taunted the leader.

Sheila began to laugh hysterically. The guerrillas looked at each other confused.

Sheila stopped laughing abruptly and looked at them. "How clichéd!" yelled Sheila. Before they could react, she jumped off the cliff backward, whipping out her pistol and firing several bullets at the grenade in the several seconds before she began to fall. The explosion filled the air as she fell down, down, the ground rushing up to meet her.

Quickly activating the parachute, her descent slowed as the parachute exploded out of the back of the jacket and caught the air. As she glided across the sky, she could see the town below. In the middle of the town, there was a small park. She put her left hand on her communicator.

"Foswell, I'm out, meet me at the park in the middle of town," she said.

"Roger that," responded Foswell.

Sheila angled the parachute towards the park. As she glided closer, she could make out a large gathering of people facing a podium on which three people stood – right where she was going to land. As she got closer, she could identify the cause for the crowd.

"Oh shit," she muttered.

Sheila angled the parachute away from the wedding, landing behind the podium. As soon as she landed, she took the jacket off and quickly rolled it and the parachute like a carpet.

She could feel that she was being watched and whipped around. The wedding party stared at her, dumbfounded. Sheila smiled and waved at the bride and groom who waved back as if in a daze. She backed away slowly, still waving and smiling, as Foswell pulled up in the jeep. The minute she was inside, they sped off.

"Is Corben …?" asked Foswell, anxiously.

"Yes, I'm sorry," Sheila said gently.

Foswell cleared his throat to choke back his emotions. He had been expecting bad news, but still … "He's in a better place," he said gruffly.

Sheila wanted to avoid details about how Corben had died or how he looked. "Are we going back to the black site?" she asked.

"No, I'm taking you back to the airport ASAP. It's too dangerous for you here. Boss's orders," answered Foswell.

"What about you?" Sheila asked.

"I'm heading back to the black site," replied Foswell as they pulled up to the plane. "They'll send another agent to join me." He bit his lip and shook his head. He hadn't just lost a partner, but a friend.

A C47 cargo plane emblazoned with the Twilight Industries logo was ready to take off. Standing on the ramp, flanked by guards holding M4A1 carbine rifles, was Connors, casually eating a doughnut.

Sheila walked up the ramp.

"Everything go alright?" Connors asked.

"Peachy," Sheila snapped. "What in the *hell* are you doing here?"

"I got tired of being behind a desk, shining a seat with my ass. So I thought I'd step into the field," Connors explained, popping the last of the doughnut into his mouth.

"I know the feeling," replied Sheila dryly as she turned around and waved goodbye to Foswell. The ramp went up, the plane lurched to life, and they flew off.

*****

News of ECHO 9's actions in Nicaragua and Russia traveled fast throughout the underworld, eventually reaching Counselor Black. He sat on the back patio of his secluded beachfront mansion in the Philippines enjoying a cup of fruit and the beautiful South Pacific sunset, having returned from dealing with ECHO 9's actions in Monaco a few days earlier.

He sat there ruminating about Project: Big Picture. If the Project was a success, then the benefit to the Networc would be unprecedented, not to mention the global implications. He had long since abandoned caring about the rest of the world; the only thing in life that had any meaning for him was the Networc, its whims and designs.

Even his years in the army felt like a dream. Life really began when he joined Applied Dynamics, ascending to the ranks of the Upper Echelon, the Networc's elite assassination and intelligence division.

He'd had a different face, eyes and hair color back then. Even different fingerprints. Everything that could be used to identify him had been destroyed, even his name. He truly was a new man. These recollections were interrupted by his cellphone ringing.

"Yes sir," he said. He'd been expecting this call.

"Progress report, Counselor Black," said Mr. Zero.

"Despite the interference of the Americans, we're still ready to proceed with Project: Big Picture, sir," replied Counselor Black.

"Excellent. And the American interlopers?" asked Mr. Zero.

"I will deal with them," replied Counselor Black. "I'll need the Lower Echelon again."

"Fine. Remember – no loose ends." Mr. Zero hung up.

Counselor Black put the phone in his pocket and resumed eating.

Chapter 13
E(vil) Mail

Finished in Russia, Simon and Deon boarded a plane and flew to an aircraft carrier in the Pacific Ocean where they were scheduled to meet Sheila. Simon and Deon were standing on the flight deck waiting for Sheila's plane to land, the old "watched pot never boils" adage coming to both their minds. They had been waiting for her on the ship for over 24 hours and were starting to get impatient. Neither would admit to fearing the worst, but conversation had been unusually low-key.

A plane glided into view above the horizon, obviously heading for the carrier. Before they knew it, it was on the deck, and the rear door opened.

Out stepped General Connors, followed by Sheila. She ran past the general to Simon and Deon.

All of Simon's worries melted when he saw her. "Hi, hon. How was Nicaragua?" he asked.

"Crashed a wedding," Sheila replied. "How about you?"

"Ate a sandwich," Simon said with a wink.

"Ahem," interrupted Connors. He stood by the entrance door. "Let's continue the reunion in the debriefing room."

"Fine," grunted Simon, irritated at the interruption.

They followed Connors into the bowels of the ship. After a long walk through the carrier's steel corridors, they arrived at the debriefing room. Four swivel chairs were positioned around a large wooden table. At the front of the room, on the wall, was a large computer screen.

Simon took off his coat, sat down in his chair, and put his feet up on the table. The others did the same. They were together. They were safe. They had survived.

"All right then, gentlemen and lady, what do we know? Sheila you go first," Connors said.

"Thank you, sir," Sheila began. As she spoke, she sounded more like an executive at a board meeting than a spy. "While my mission in Castoňa was not as fruitful as I had hoped, I did discover that whatever the Networc's goal is, it's known as Project: Big Picture. The man in charge is known as Counselor Black; present location, the Philippines."

"All right then, what about you two?" Connors asked.

"According to Menshov, the Networc has a considerable interest in a Belarusian facility known as Sanction Blue. They've been storing and developing nuclear, chemical, and biological weapons," Deon said.

Connors face and body suddenly went rigid.

"You know where it is, don't you?" Simon asked, already knowing the answer.

"Yes I do. It's located smack dab in the middle of the country dealing with one hell of a civil war," Connors said.

"Figures," Simon said, rolling his eye.

"Wait a sec; how the hell did you find the place so fast?" Sheila asked.

"We've always known about it," Connors said quietly.

"What?" Deon sat up in surprise.

"I *knew* it! You knew about this the whole time didn't you?" Simon said angrily. "You always have an angle, Connors."

"There's no angle," Connors said.

"Bull," said Simon.

"Despite what you think, I'm telling the truth," Connors explained. "We've known about Sanction Blue since 1975 when they built it. And yes, we've been watching it ever since. But – and it's an important 'but' – we never thought something like this could happen," continued Connors.

"Uh huh," replied Simon dismissively.

"My question is – where do the guns come in?" Deon asked.

Connors shrugged. "We don't know, but my suspicions were correct. This is clearly much bigger than some missing guns. What concerns me is what these people have in mind for Sanction Blue."

"Obviously, we need more intel. What about this Counselor Black guy? Sheila said he's in the Philippines," suggested Deon.

As if in response, the phone that connected them to the bridge rang. Connors picked up the receiver. As he listened, his expression changed to one of surprise. "Understood," said Connors, putting the phone down.

"Come with me to the bridge," ordered Connors sternly.

"Why? What happened?" Simon took his feet off the table.

"The Networc just sent us a message," Connors said cryptically as he walked out the door.

When they got to the bridge the ship's captain, Allen Fairchild, greeted them.

"Welcome to the bridge; it's a pleasure to finally meet you all," said the Captain warmly, shaking their hands.

"Likewise, I'm sure," Simon said.

Connors was impatient. "Now then, what's this business message about?" he asked.

"Follow me." They followed Fairchild to his office down the hall from the bridge. It was well furnished with a wooden desk, computer, and three chairs. Fairchild sat behind the desk while Connors and Deon sat in the two chairs in front of the desk.

"Comfy," Deon said as he leaned back in the chair.

Fairchild pulled a bottle of gin and four shot glasses out of a drawer. "I know you spooks have a fetish for secrecy, so I figured you'd want to see this in private. I also figured that a drink would help with the jet lag," said the captain as he poured some gin into the glasses before putting the bottle back in the drawer.

"No thanks," Simon said, trying not to look at the bottle.

"Speak for yourself, Simon," Deon said. He and Connors grabbed their glasses and tossed them back.

"Can we get down to business now?" Sheila said impatiently, also ignoring the offered drink.

"Of course. while you were debriefing, I happened to be checking my e-mails when I received this," said the captain as he turned the computer around and showed them the message on the monitor.

The four of them gathered close to read it:

Silhouette, we of the Neutral Executive for Total World Order Regardless of Consequence do not tolerate foreign interference in our affairs. However, we are reasonable people and are willing to negotiate a deal that will avoid any further violence. Enclosed are the coordinates of my mansion in the Philippines. If you wish to discuss this matter further, be there within the next four days.

- Counselor Black

"Well, at least we know why it's called the Networc," Deon said dryly.

"What is it with bad guys and acronyms?" asked Simon drily.

"How the hell do they know about us in the first place?" Sheila asked anxiously.

Connors was confident in the team. "All questions that you will make him answer," he said.

Simon reared up, indignant. "Are you out of your goddamn mind? It's a trap!" he exclaimed.

"It's also our first real shot at finding these bastards," Connors said calmly. "Besides, you're not going there to talk."

"Meaning ..." Sheila began.

"Meaning that this has gone on long enough. I'm sending you to execute a blackout maneuver," answered Connors.

Simon, Sheila, and Deon exchanged looks. Blackout maneuver was a term they knew all too well. It was the code name for a mission requiring them to kill a target.

Connors looked at Fairchild. "How close are we to those coordinates?"

"I can have a plane ready to fly you there in eight hours," answered Fairchild.

"Make it four. While you're doing that, we'll be prepping for the op," replied Connors.

Chapter 14
Hostile Negotiators

Counselor Black's mansion was surrounded on three sides by dense forest and on one by the ocean. During their briefings, the team decided that the best course of action would be to take a helicopter with a Zodiac boat on board, drop the boat in the water off the coast of his estate, and enter the mansion. As they proceeded, the helicopter would fly back to the carrier, and await a signal to pick them up again.

It was dark by the time they arrived at the beach. They left the boat on the beach and cocked their weapons.

Simon was using a Heckler and Koch 416, Deon was carrying an M4A1 carbine with an underbarrel M203 grenade launcher, and Sheila was using a Heckler and Koch MP5. They each wore standard issue Silhouette combat gear: black turtleneck, gloves, long black pants. They each wore a brown belt. On their chests was a brown harness with a shoulder holster and several clips that various items could be attached to, if necessary. In this case, the clips had magazines attached to them. Slung over their shoulders were their rifles.

Simon pointed to the mansion and made a thumbs-up sign. The others nodded in agreement. Sign language made stealth that much easier. They slowly walked up the beach and onto the rear patio, past a pool before stacking up beside the sliding doors. Simon motioned to Sheila to try them. She walked slowly to the door; the door were unlocked and slid silently open. The others followed her inside.

They appeared to be in a living room dominated by a massive TV screen. To its right and left were massive wooden shelves filled with books. The walls were decorated with fine art. They checked the house thoroughly from the bedroom on the second floor to the wine cellar in the basement.

They met back in the living room, confused and irritated, when suddenly the TV came to life. On the screen was the face of, apparently, Counselor Black. His face was plain with piercing brown eyes and dark black hair.

"Looking for me?" Counselor Black asked smugly.

"Hey, guys I found him," Deon said sarcastically.

"Indeed you have, Sgt. Bowman."

Deon wasn't expecting that. "How do you know my name?"

"We know all your names. Or would you prefer to be called by your code name, ROUNDABOUT?" Counselor Black asked arrogantly.

"When you sent us that invitation, we thought we'd be talking to *you*, not to a TV screen," Simon said.

"Sadly, at the moment I'm miles away on a private flight to Minsk, Mr. Kane. Though I must say it's both a pleasure and a shame to vanquish opponents as formidable as you three. Alas, the final curtain is about to fall on our little drama" said Counselor Black, fairly oozing with self-appreciation.

"We ain't dead yet, you arrogant lunatic," Sheila barked defiantly.

"Ahh, Americans, no sense of drama," Black crooned.

"I'll make sure those words are engraved on your tombstone, Miss *Goodbody*, interesting last name by the way," continued Counselor Black.

"Better than yours" grunted Sheila.

"You know, it's customary to grant the condemned a last request," said Simon.

"True. I see no reason to deny you that request. What is it?" asked Counselor Black.

"Since we're going to die anyway," Simon said, "tell us what Project: Big Picture is."

Counselor Black laughed. "A splendid request. After all, it is perhaps the most audacious heist in history." Black leaned a little closer to the camera. "We intend to use the guns we stole from *you* to steal the *nuclear* weapons from Sanction Blue."

"Why?" Sheila asked.

Counselor Black shrugged. "Because they are too dangerous to be in the hands of those who don't respect them," answered Black.

"And who the hell gave you the right to make that decision" asked Simon.

"That's a question for my superiors," replied Black smugly.

"And they would be …?" Simon ventured. *As long as he likes to talk, why not ask?*

"You won't live long enough to find out. None of you will," Black said with a smile.

Deon took a step toward the screen. "Whether we're alive or dead, there's no way in hell you'll be able to get anywhere near Sanction Blue. The whole country is tearing itself to pieces," he said.

Counselor Black chuckled ominously. "Who do you think started that civil war in the first place, Sgt. Bowman?"

"What are you saying?" Simon asked.

"Through the careful manipulation of the political and economic machine, we provoked the Belarusian civil war," said Counselor Black.

"It's not like your country hasn't done it before, and for the record, neither have we," Counselor Black continued.

"Now then, you have been granted your last requests, and I must say goodbye. Or as they say in Belarus, *da pabačeńnya!*" said Counselor Black.

The TV abruptly switched off; an ominous quiet filled the room.

"Anybody else got a bad feeling about this?" Deon muttered, on the alert.

"No, you?" answered Sheila.

"Nah," replied Deon.

"What about you, Simon?" Deon asked.

"Not really," replied Simon.

"I'm calling the boss anyway," continued Simon. "NARRATOR, this is MONOLITH, did you catch all that?" All he could get on the radio was static.

Simon looked up at Sheila and Deon. "Guys, it just got worse. I can't contact Connors."

"Well...shit," said Deon bluntly.

"They must be jamming us," Sheila said.

"So now what?" Deon inquired.

Simon grimaced. "We get the hell out of here."

"Damn, and I just got comfortable," said Deon sarcastically.

Suddenly, their radios buzzed and crackled to life.

"ECHO 9, come in, come in!" radioed Connors.

"Roger that, NARRATOR. Go ahead," Simon said.

"Be advised. We've detected an unidentified predator drone preparing to fire on your position. Take cover, over." The radio cut out again.

"You were saying, Deon?" Sheila said dryly.

Simon looked out the window and into the sky. *Where is it? Something ... just barely visible ...*"Take cover!" he yelled.

The three scrambled to find some semblance of safety from the impending missile. A minute later, the compound was inundated with fire, smoke, and rubble.

Thousands of miles away in an executive office, the enigmatic leader of the Networc known only as Mr. Zero watched the whole thing in real time on his computer screen. He smiled slyly as the missile hit the building. "Ashes to ashes and dust to dust," he said.

Chapter 15
When the Dust Settles

Simon was the first to wake up. Though dazed, he quickly recovered his senses. He looked around and saw Sheila's lifeless body. His first thought was that she had been killed in the blast. He ran to her praying that he was wrong. Suddenly she began to cough, standing up shakily. Simon breathed a sigh of relief as Deon stood up as well. Their faces were covered in dust and rubble.

"You okay?" Simon asked.

"Do I look okay?" snapped Sheila sarcastically.

Simon grinned at her comeback. "Well, you have looked better," he said.

Deon and Sheila laughed slightly at the wisecrack despite their predicament.

"The real question is *how* are we still alive?" Sheila asked as she rubbed her head.

"Remember? Just before the missile hit, we sprinted to that door with the stairs leading here. We ran in just before the missile hit," Deon explained.

"Well, that answers the 'how' – what about the 'where'?" Simon pulled a pen-sized flashlight out of his belt and turned it on. As the beam traveled all over the area, it landed on three rows of shelves at the far end of the room filled with bottles. "It's the wine cellar!" he exclaimed.

"Yeah, I'd cleared it earlier while you two were roaming the house. I guess wine is good for you after all," Deon quipped.

"That's one way of looking at it," Simon agreed.

Deon pulled out his flashlight as well, waving it around, searching for a way out.

"At least we're not trapped down here," he said, discovering stairs on the other side of the room.

"Grab your gear and let's get out of here!" Simon took the lead as they made it up the stairs, glad to be away from the wine.

The door was blocked by rubble, but they managed to move the rubble aside. As soldiers, they had seen tremendous destruction, but even they were shocked at the level of devastation. The once-opulent and beautiful mansion had been reduced to a pile of smoking rubble. They walked through what was left of the living room and back to the beach.

In the quiet of the morning, the sound of a gun being cocked got their attention.

"Did you guys hear that?" whispered Sheila.

Simon and Deon nodded. Simon held up his hand and pointed to the left and right walls signaling for them to take cover. They stood silent, tensed, ready for anything. They tried to determine where, exactly, the sound had come from.

The sun was barely up and the rustling of the trees in the wind made it hard to triangulate the click's location, even harder to confirm whether it was a gun at all. They were sure it was, but …

The seconds passed like hours. Suddenly Deon detected faint footsteps approaching from their rear and pointed to what was left of the front door. The others nodded. They dove for cover just as several armed gunmen burst through the emaciated charred remains of the mansion's front door carrying assault rifles.

"Deon, get the boat ready!" yelled Simon as he and Sheila turned around to fire at the gunmen, all the while slowly backing toward the boat.

"Think I'd let you have all the fun?" Sheila replied.

"The more the merrier," muttered Simon as they fired at them.

They managed to hit several of the attackers in the head with their initial barrage. The remaining gunmen took cover behind the walls.

"Who are these assholes?" yelled Sheila over the cacophonous gunfire.

"Must be the mop-up crew," answered Deon.

"I'll give them this, the bastards are thorough!" shouted Simon.

Over the staccato of hot lead flying back and forth, a boat engine growled to life. "Guys! The train is leaving!" yelled Deon.

"You heard the man, last train to Clarksville," Simon called to Sheila. They turned and ran toward the boat.

As they ran, the soldiers realized that they were no longer under fire. They began to peek out from cover and shoot at the fleeing trio. Reaching the boat, Simon pulled out five coins, pressed the edges, and tossed them at the mansion. The coins landed on the ground in front of the shooters, who looked at them confused, as if wondering if they should pick them up. As Simon and Sheila jumped in the boat, the coins exploded, killing most of the remaining shooters.

"Penny for your thoughts," Simon said loudly as they pulled away from the mansion.

"Dude really?" Deon just glared at him.

Simon grinned with a shrug. "What? It was too easy."

On shore, the leader of the gunmen pulled out his phone and dialed the number of Counselor Black. After a few rings, Counselor Black picked up.

"Is it done, Voller?" Counselor Black asked.

"I'm sorry, sir. Somehow the Americans managed to not only survive but also escape from me and my men."

Counselor Black sighed long and loud. "Understood. A gunship is en route to your position to give chase."

"Yes sir," replied Voller as the phone went silent.

The sun was just beginning to rise by the time Simon, Sheila, and Deon reached the rendezvous point where the helicopter was supposed to pick them up. The ocean was as flat as glass, an endless mirror in the morning sunlight. They had been waiting for almost a half an hour and still couldn't contact Connors or the carrier.

Sheila and Deon slept while Simon kept watch for the chopper. He was starting to fall asleep, despite his best efforts, when suddenly he heard the unmistakable sound of an approaching helicopter engine. He was about to waken Deon and Sheila when it occurred to him that the chopper was coming from an unexpected direction. Quickly he picked up his rifle and looked through the ACOG scope to get a better look.

The sight stopped his heart for a beat. It was a Russian Hind D gunship with rocket pods and a mini-gun.

"Oh, shit," Simon grunted.

Simon's mind raced to think of a possible way out of this, but nothing was coming. The chopper, on the other hand, was coming at a very fast rate, closer and closer by the second. Simon accelerated the engine in a desperate attempt to get away from it.

Sheila and Deon woke up at the jolt, but before they could ask what was going on, Simon pointed to the chopper behind them.

"Oh," Deon said.

"Crap," Sheila said.

Suddenly, the helicopter's speed increased and it opened fire on them with its mini-gun. Simon pulled a hard right, maneuvering out of the way of the deadly salvo. He accelerated as fast as they could while the helicopter followed like a hunter closing in for the kill.

"What's he doing? One missile would kill us like that!" Deon said, snapping his fingers.

"The sick bastard's toying with us," Simon said.

Just then, the helicopter fired another mini-gun fusillade that barely missed them. Simon responded by moving forward in a serpentine pattern in a desperate attempt to evade getting hit. Sheila and Deon fired at the chopper to no avail.

Switching tactics, the helicopter fired a rocket that exploded in front of them, flipping the boat and knocking them into the water. They instinctively swam to the surface, only to be greeted by the chopper. It looked like an enormous animal ready to pounce on its prey.

"Well guys, it's been fun, but I'd say we're officially dead," Sheila yelled, the sarcasm unable to completely mask her concern.

"Speak for yourselves," Deon shouted over the noise of the propellers.

"What makes you so damn special?" yelled Sheila.

"I'm a Marine, Marines, don't die – they just go to hell and regroup," Deon shouted back at her.

Simon and Sheila looked at him, not sure how to react to his comment.

"Good thing I joined the Army!" Sheila quipped.

Simon and Deon cracked a smile at Sheila's joke. *When you're screwed, the only thing you can do is laugh in the face of death.* Simon put his arm around Sheila and gazed into her eyes. "I love you, hon," Simon said.

"Ditto, One Eye," she responded.

Deon swam closer to them. "We'll see you on the other side, Deon," Simon told him.

Deon flashed a smile and gave them both a sarcastic salute.

In the next second, the helicopter was engulfed in a massive explosion. They ducked instinctively, but when they surfaced, the helicopter was gone. Pieces floated all around. Turning toward the sound of engines, they saw two helicopters hovering above them – one was an American Sea Knight and the other was an AH-64 Apache attack helicopter.

As they watched, the reality of their rescue began to dawn on them. A rope ladder descended from the Sea Knight, and they climbed into the chopper. Once they were all inside the choppers turned around and began the long flight back to the carrier.

Chapter 16
Operation: SAVAGE GARDEN

Bruised, battered, and waterlogged from their mission to the Philippines, ECHO 9 was now safely back on the carrier. Upon landing, they were rushed to the ship's medical bay and remarkably, despite a few bumps, cuts, and scratches, none of them was seriously injured. Connors, realizing that they were in no condition to debrief after their mission, ordered them to get some R&R for the next few hours in the cabins the ship's captain provided. In the meantime, Connors would analyze their intel.

The next morning they met in the briefing room ready and willing to get back to the job. They were dressed in their more traditional garb, Simon in his trench coat with black button-down and dark green pants, Deon with a yellow short-sleeved shirt and black pants. Sheila had on her favorite ensemble – black shirt, white pants and black leather jacket. They wouldn't win any fashion contests, but all in all, they looked none the worse for wear.

On the middle of the table were coffee and donuts. Simon sat at the end of the table and poured himself a cup of coffee, half-and-half and two sugars. Sheila sat on the left, grateful for the coffee, while Deon, on the right, grabbed two jelly donuts. A few minutes later, Connors walked in and stood at the front of the table. Behind him was the computer screen.

"Good morning," Connors said.

"What's so good about it?" Sheila quipped.

"Before we start, I'll ask what we're all wondering. Specifically how did you know we were still alive after that missile hit?" Simon asked.

Connors smiled smugly. "C'mon. We all know you three have survived rougher missions than that. I just took it on faith … and infrared satellite imaging."

"Always helps to have an eye in the sky," said Simon as he held up his cup in mock salute to the general.

"Are you up to speed on what the Networc is planning?" Sheila asked.

"Yes, despite the Networc's best efforts to the contrary," answered Connors, realizing by their confused faces that an explanation was in order. "While your communicators were being jammed we managed to isolate their coms signal and listen to their transmissions. Unfortunately, we could not track it back to its source."

"So where does that leave us?" Deon asked. Simon caught his eye and licked the side of his own mouth – Deon wiped the offending jelly from his face.

"Simple. We go after them. As bad as those rifles they stole are, the contents of Sanction Blue are much worse. We cannot allow them to be distributed across the globe," Connors grimaced.

"While I'm sure we all agree with you, I think you're overlooking a certain undeniable facet of this course of action," Simon said.

Connors sighed, knowing what was coming. "Just for the sake of argument, enlighten me," he said.

"Belarus!" Simon shook his head. "The whole damn country is tearing itself apart in civil war. Hell, just getting in there without getting shot would be next to impossible. *If* we got inside, we'd have to contend with both the rebels and the Belarusian army, long before we reached the bunker," answered Simon.

"Already taken care of," Connors said.

"How?" Deon asked.

Connors had a "tell," a certain Cheshire cat grin he made whenever a difficult mission such as this required extreme cunning and guile. The team had seen it before and knew exactly what it meant. Usually, it wasn't a good sign, and he had it now.

"I don't like the looks of this," Deon muttered.

Connors pulled the remote control for the screen out of his pocket. Aiming it at the screen, he pressed a button. A satellite map of Belarus appeared on the screen; on the lower left corner of the map near the Polish border was a blue circle.

"That blue circle represents Sanction Blue's exact location. Fortunately for us it's not located near any highly populated areas," continued Connors.

"So what's the plan?" Sheila asked.

"Ah yes, the plan. Crossing the border would take too long, with too much of a fight. You'll be doing an air insertion." Connors paused for the inevitable backlash.

"That's insane!" Simon exclaimed. "The rebels will shoot down any American plane that enters Belarusian airspace!"

"True," Connors agreed. "But who said anything about using an American military plane?"

"Go on … we're intrigued," Sheila said.

"You'll be entering Belarus via a UN private jet," Connors said.

"The UN?" Deon said, echoing the mild surprise of Sheila and Simon. Even if the United Nations knew about Silhouette's existence there was no way in the UN would help them.

"Perhaps I should explain," said Connors smoothly. "The UN is currently trying to negotiate peace talks with both sides of the Belarusian civil war. They're flying over several diplomats to lead the peace talks. However," he paused for effect, "at the last minute I made sure the plane they were going to use was deemed unsafe. They were generously given a new plane, courtesy of Silhouette – a plane complete with UN identification that will fly to Minsk in three days from JFK," he said.

"Soooo...?" Deon said.

Connors loved to drag out the details, keeping them on the edge of their seats.

"The plane is identical to the original, with one exception: Under the cargo hold is a hidden chamber containing the necessary equipment for you to parachute out of the plane when you get the signal," explained Connors.

Typical Connors, audacious and underhanded. Also brilliant, thought Simon.

"Ingenious," Sheila nodded.

"So the UN actually *is* good for something." Deon said sarcastically.

"Imagine that," Simon deadpanned.

"Yeah, yeah, we're all very impressed, Connors, but once the mission is done, how do we get *out* of the country?"

"Once you've destroyed the facility you'll have to fight your way to the Polish border and sneak through. As you can see, it isn't that far from Sanction Blue," Connors said.

"Figures," grunted Simon.

"Hold on, how are we supposed to destroy it?" Deon asked.

"Sanction Blue is mostly underground. Once inside you'll fight your way to the central control room and activate the compound's DE-CON protocol," Connors said.

"DE-CON protocol?" Simon said. "What the fuck is that?"

"A code the Russians developed in case something went wrong and they had to eliminate all traces of the facility. Essentially, once you type it into the bunker's central computer, it'll activate the bunker's self-destruct sequence, and before you ask, Simon, yes we have the code," explained Connors.

"Assuming we have one, what's our cover on the plane?" Deon asked. Knowing Connors, he might expect them to hole up in the cargo space, freezing their butts off.

"You'll be posing as three American journalists covering the peace talks," Connors answered.

"Of course, there's much more to this – it's all covered in the mission dossier."

"Why all the cloak-and-dagger bullshit? Why not send in a B-2 and hit the place with a few bunker busters?" Simon asked.

"Too high profile. The president made it clear that we can't afford an international incident in Belarus. An American airstrike would turn a shitty situation into a shittier one. Besides, the bunkers have been reinforced to withstand being hit with anything short of a nuke. We're calling this Operation: SAVAGE GARDEN," said Connors.

"Like the band?" asked Sheila.

"Band?" Deon was confused.

"Yeah, from Australia. Don't you listen to music?" replied Simon.

"I listen to music … *good* music," replied Deon.

"If you're all *quite* done? The mission? I want to make one thing crystal clear before you go: Of all the missions I've sent you on, this one is much different. The stakes have never been higher. These people – the Networc – are not like the people you fought with Silhouette before," began Connors.

"From what we've been able to gather, their forces used to be members of some of the deadliest Special Forces teams in the world. They are as highly trained and well equipped as you three, and there's a lot more of them. So good luck," continued Connors.

The team let Connors' words sink in. With Silhouette, they fought terrorists, spies, even whole armies, but they had never fought an adversary as powerful and cunning as the Networc. It was as though they were staring at their reflections in a cracked mirror. Anyone else would cower in the face of such an enemy, but as they looked at one another, they knew that of anyone in the world, the three people formerly known as ECHO 9 were up for the challenge.

Simon detected the slight nods from his partners. "Connors, I think I speak for all of us when I ask, 'When do we leave?'"

"Hell, yeah," Deon said.

"Damn straight," Sheila agreed.

Connors smiled. He had seen the same determined bravado on the faces of his brothers-in-arms in Vietnam, and when he left the battlefield to become, decades later, a leader behind a conference room desk, he'd seen it countless times there as well. Connors was relieved at the reaction, though. Any doubts he may have felt about the team's effectiveness just vanished. "Tonight, 1900 hours. Good luck," he said.

As they boarded the plane that would fly them to New York that night, they found dossiers on their seats along with changes of clothes, tasteful and professional as befitting world-class journalists. Written on the cover of the dossiers were the words "Operation: SAVAGE GARDEN" in black.

Chapter 17
The Diplomats

After a 24-hour flight, Simon, Deon and Sheila arrived at JFK airport in New York. Simon had once again used Janusum and sunglasses to disguise himself. Exiting the plane, they were greeted by a tall man in a suit.

"How was the flight?" he asked.

"Too long. And you are?" Simon asked.

"Clapton, Twilight Industries," the man explained.

"Of course you are," Simon muttered, crankier than usual from the flight.

"Where's our plane?" Sheila asked, looking around.

"It's on the tarmac waiting. My orders are to take you to it now," replied Clapton.

"Lead on, Kemosabe," Deon said.

They followed Clapton through the airport to the tarmac in a restricted area. It was starting to rain by the time they got there. Simon, Sheila, and Deon walked up the movable stairway to the plane, and the door closed behind them. They were shown to their seats by a smiling flight attendant.

After a few minutes, the captain's voice buzzed over the intercom and announced that they were now ready for take-off. Simon wondered how the civilian passengers would react if they knew that the entire flight crew, including the two pilots, were Silhouette agents in disguise. Given the level of expertise the agents represented, they'd probably feel safer.

Until they found out why, he thought as the plane barreled down the runway for its thirteen-hour flight.

Once they were in the air, Simon turned around to the seat behind him and saw that Sheila and Deon were already sound asleep. Yawning, he turned back around. *If you can't beat 'em, join 'em.* The hum of the engine soon put him to sleep as well.

Several hours later, they were awakened by one of the flight attendants, who invited them to follow her to the cockpit. She knocked on the door lightly. The co-pilot opened it and they walked in; the flight attendant returned to her duties.

"So you're the infamous ECHO 9," said the captain as he shook their hands in turn from his seat.

"What's ECHO 9?" Deon asked sarcastically.

The captain chuckled. "I love a sense of humor, especially in our line of work. Call me Captain Lee," he said with a smile. "Not my name, you understand, but I'll answer to it."

"What's the plan?" Sheila asked.

"We'll be over the drop zone in 30 minutes, so get ready. Your gear's in the parachute bay," "Captain Lee" answered.

"Thanks," Simon said, turning to leave.

"Wait – before you go take this." The captain pulled a Phillips head screwdriver from his jacket's inner pocket and lightly tossed it to Simon. "Good luck," he said.

Simon looked at the sleeping passengers and then back at the captain. "Thanks, you too," said Simon.

Sheila and Deon were already standing outside of the bathroom at the end of the plane. "What took you so long?" Deon asked.

"Had to get the key," Simon said as he held up the screwdriver.

"Good thing all the passengers are asleep," Sheila whispered as she opened the door.

"Otherwise they might think we're coming in here together to have a 'Mile-High Club' threesome," she said.

It was a tight squeeze inside, but Simon knelt down in front of the toilet, and unscrewed a square panel in front of the commode. Once it was loose enough, he removed it. A small ladder led into a narrow hallway beneath them.

Simon gestured to Sheila. "Ladies first."

"So … go on," joked Sheila.

Deon laughed softly at them. He wondered how long it would take before someone complained about the *occupied* sign on the door.

Sheila climbed down the ladder..

"Damn, she got you man," Deon teased, easing himself through the opening.

"Me? I thought she meant you!" said Simon as he followed Deon down the ladder. He screwed the panel back in with the special two-way screws before following his comrades into the cramped hallway. At the end was a small room containing two unmarked crates on opposite sides of the room. Between the crates was Sheila. Directly across was a little door.

"Before we go any further, Simon, will you please take off those goofy sunglasses?" Sheila asked sweetly.

Simon grinned and shrugged his shoulders, removing both the sunglasses and the Janusum, and pulling his trusty eyepatch from his pocket. He rubbed his hands together. "Let's get down to business!"

"Hell yeah," Deon and Sheila said together.

The crate on the right contained their combat gear and equipment. "Finally we can ditch these monkey suits," Sheila said gleefully

They undressed and put on the black stealth suits, parachutes, belts, and holsters, stuffing the other clothes back in the crate.

"Time for the party favors," Deon said, as they shifted their attention to the other crate.

Simon opened the crate of weapons. Sheila pulled out a scoped M4A1 carbine with an under-barrel grenade launcher and five magazines, her Walther P99 pistol and three magazines, and, for good measure, a knife. Simon pulled out his Jericho 941 along with five magazines, his scoped Heckler and Koch 416 assault rifles with ammo, a knife, and several grenades. Deon pulled out his M9 Beretta and silenced MK13 sniper rifle, ammo, knife, grenades.

"Everyone ready?" Simon said.

Deon finished putting things in various places on his body. "I'd say we're loaded for bear."

Sheila nodded in agreement.

"All right, let's make the magic happen," Simon said, opening the door behind them.

A minute later, a loud buzzing noise above them signaled that it was time to go. Simon flipped a switch; the wall in front of them slid open inundating them with cold night air. Below, pitch-blackness hid the carnage below. They each took a deep breath and jumped.

As they parachuted down, Simon glanced upward at the plane and wondered who the real diplomats were: the UN ambassadors on the plane or he and his black ops team parachuting through the inky sky?

Chapter 18
The Hornet's Nest

The team landed in a clearing in the woods. After silently checking to see if they were all okay, they hid their parachutes, cocked their weapons, and put on their night vision goggles. Simon pulled a small GPS out of his pocket to see how far away the compound was. He motioned to the others and pointed to the woods.

In front of him, Sheila and Deon got the message. They followed him through the woods for two hours, surreptitiously, guns drawn.

Suddenly, they heard the unmistakable pop of a gunshot nearby. Freezing in their tracks, they waited. None of them had been hit and no one else was moving. Sheila made a pistol with her hand.

Simon and Deon nodded in agreement. Makarov pistols were the most common weapon for both sides in the civil war. Deon pointed to his left, the direction of the shot, suggesting they follow it. Simon gave the universal "OK" before heading into the brush.

The closer they walked, the better they could detect voices speaking Russian. A clearing was ahead. They stopped just outside of it, hiding in the bushes. A group of five men stood by a truck. Two were on their knees; two were standing. One had a pistol aimed at the head of one of the men on the ground. Deon instinctively raised his sniper rifle and aimed it at the man with the gun.

Simon put his hand on the barrel of the gun. Deon was confused but Simon whispered.

"It's not our fight; we have a choice – save one or save millions."

Deon reluctantly lowered his rifle. He followed Simon and Sheila as they continued on the path to Sanction Blue, ignoring the shots they heard behind them. Simon knew he'd made the right call, avoiding detection so early in the mission, but he hated it nevertheless.

Several hours later, the sun was starting to rise. Night goggles had long since been put away. Approaching the edge of the forest, they could finally see their objective, Sanction Blue.

A small concrete building with a solid steel door was the only indication that anything of note was there. Two armed Networc mercenaries patrolled the front of the door. Next to the building were three black unmarked armored trucks.

Sheila pulled out her binoculars and studied the area.

"Well?" whispered Simon.

"I count two hostiles standing outside the entrance, both armed with the stolen super guns and body armor," she answered.

"Don't worry about the armor; I'll aim for the head," whispered Deon confidently.

"Okay, here's the plan: Sheila and I will go in while you provide cover, deal?" whispered Simon.

They nodded. "Do your stuff," whispered Sheila, pointing to the two guards.

"Not a problem, ma'am," Deon said as he looked through the sight of his silenced rifle.

He fired two rounds, hitting both guards in the head.

"I hope it's all that easy," whispered Sheila as the lifeless bodies fell onto the green grass, knowing it wouldn't be.

Sheila and Simon sprinted across the field towards the bunker entrance. Sheila opened the door and followed Simon inside. Once in, they stood atop a stairwell that led into the bowels of the compound where their main objective waited below. They felt as though they were staring into the inner circle of hell itself.

Gingerly they walked down the dimly lit stairs, silently praying they were not too late. At the bottom of the stairs was a solid steel door with worn Russian inscriptions. Sheila and Simon looked at each other grimly, wondering how many men were waiting on the other side. Even though the door was old, it would be strong enough to hold off enemy fire; they could use it as a shield if needed.

Sheila stayed behind Simon as he reached for the handle, slowly pulling it open just enough to peer out. Greeted by a barrage of gunfire, he quickly withdrew behind the door. "I don't think we're welcome here, hon. I saw three of them, and they aren't friendly."

"Damn! And I got all dressed up too!" Sheila said sarcastically. She pulled a flash-bang from her grenade belt and tossed it out the door. They covered their ears as it exploded, stunning the three gunmen with a combination of loud noise and blinding light. With only a few seconds to act, they swung open the door and fired several rounds at the gunmen, killing them.

They took a few minutes to study their surroundings. They were at the end of a long hallway with multiple doors on both sides. At the end was a door, which according to their admittedly dated map was the only thing separating them from their objective.

"These goons probably aren't the only ones down here," Simon said stepping over the three dead men.

"Better hurry then," Sheila said casually.

Simon and Sheila ran down the hallway, not even wanting to guess what kind of monstrous weapons were behind the doors to their left and right. Suddenly, two gunmen ran out of a door to the left of the control room door, aiming their rifles at Simon and Sheila.

Simon and Sheila looked at each other. "High," Simon said.

"Low," Sheila replied.

Sheila ran to gather momentum before dropping to her knees and sliding along the tile floor as she shot one of the gunmen in the chest, while Simon ran at top speed right for the men, shooting the other in the head. Simon helped Sheila up; they slowly approached the control room door. Sheila opened it and headed straight for the main console. Simon followed – the next part was all Sheila.

Sheila quickly typed in the code. "Almost got it," she said tersely.

"Let's hope you don't," said a voice behind her.

Sheila froze; she recognized the voice – the man who'd almost killed them in the Philippines. She turned around stiffly. Counselor Black had his right arm around Simon's neck while his left hand aimed a gun at Simon's head. Simon appeared to be unconscious.

"For *his* sake, that is," said Counselor Black smugly.

Chapter 19
In the Blink of an Eye

"It's a pleasure to finally meet you both in person," continued Counselor Black as if addressing party guests.

Instinctively, Sheila drew her pistol and aimed it at Counselor Black's head. "Let him go," she growled.

Counselor Black sighed. "Seeing as how you've been outmaneuvered in this little chess game of ours, can we please dispense with the clichéd histrionics?" said Counselor Black.

Sheila's mind raced to come up with a way out of this. There was nothing she could do while he used Simon's body as a shield. Was there? Her only option was to shoot Simon and hope that the bullet had enough power to travel through him and hit Counselor Black, killing them both in the process.

I can't kill the only man I ever loved. As she cursed herself for her sentimentality, Simon winked with his one eye. In that second, she understood his plan. *Just like in Rio* she thought

"How about we dispense with you instead?" Sheila asked.

Simon jammed his elbow into Counselor Black's stomach, causing him to drop his gun and loosen the grip on his neck. Free again, Simon swung around and knocked him to the ground with a left uppercut.

Simon stood over Black and looked at Sheila. "Just like in Rio, eh hon?" Simon said, grinning.

"Yep, only in reverse," Sheila said, shaking her head.

"I'll handle him, you punch in the codes," said Simon.

Sheila nodded and ran back to the console to resume entering the DE-CON code. Simon turned just in time to get punched in the face by Counselor Black.

"I will not be 'handled.'" he said defiantly.

Simon jumped out of reach with a smile. "Just what I wanted to hear. It's been too long since I've had a good fight," said Simon.

Simon dodged and tried to counter with a blow to the stomach. Black caught the punch in his left hand and squeezed it hard.

"Hell of a grip," Simon muttered, trying not to show pain.

Counselor Black smiled before head-butting Simon and kicking him in the stomach.

Ignoring the searing sensations in his head and stomach, Simon pulled out his Jericho 941. *Fuck it* thought Simon. Before he could pull the trigger, however, Counselor Black grabbed him by his shirt, kicked him again in the stomach, and threw him against the wall.

Simon fell to the ground. "That all you got?" Simon gasped.

"You people have been worthy adversaries, but I'm afraid it's time to enter the next world," said Counselor Black menacingly as he picked up Simon by his shirt collar.

"You first," growled Simon.

Suddenly, the room was filled with noise and light as an alarm blared and siren lights blinked red.

"Self-destruct sequence has commenced," a voice came over the loudspeaker in clipped Russian.

"Checkmate, asshole," Simon said, grinning in victory.

Enraged at seeing the fruit of years of planning snatched away from him, Counselor Black threw Simon down to the ground. He picked up Simon's pistol, whipped around, and aimed it at Sheila's forehead and pulled the trigger.

Her body quickly fell to the floor, but to Simon, her body fell in slow motion. The sound of the gunshot reverberated throughout the underground base as if to sound her death knell.

Simon's years of training told him that she was dead before she hit the floor, but the shock was overwhelming. The love of his life was gone forever. And standing in front of him was the man who had darkened the light in her eyes. His grief and shock turned to rage when he noticed the smug smile of satisfaction on her killer's face.

"Don't worry, you'll be joining her soon," Counselor Black told him as he gloated over his victim.

In that moment, Simon was overcome with seething rage and vengeance. With the speed and strength of a man possessed, he jumped to his feet and grabbed Counselor Black from behind. He wrapped his hands around his head. "Damn you," growled Simon in a voice that sounded like the devil himself. He snapped Black's neck with a sickening crack.

Watching Counselor Black's lifeless body fall to the floor did nothing to quell his rage or his grief.at. He staggered over to her body, tears beginning to form in his eyes. He fell to his knees beside her as his tears mingled with her blood on the floor. Even with the gaping hole in her forehead, she looked strangely peaceful.

Simon picked up her torso and held her in his arms. They had hoped to resume their life together after this hellish mission, a shattered dream. For one flickering instant, Simon contemplated killing himself so he could be with Sheila in eternity, but a thought suddenly occurred to him: the organization that her killer worked for still existed, still thrived, still schemed.

If he died, Sheila's death would be for nothing, would go unavenged. That was unacceptable. The people who caused her death must face justice. Suddenly he remembered the countdown – avenging her would only be possible if he left immediately.

"I'll make them pay Sheila, I promise," vowed Simon as he held her one last time.

Kissing her goodbye, he stood up and wiped the tears from his face. *She won't even get the burial she deserves* thought Simon. He grabbed his Jericho and looked at Counselor Black's body. He spit on his face and sprinted out of the control room, down the hallway, and up the stairs while the countdown continued. Once outside, he dashed across the field to Deon's location.

"Take cover!" yelled Simon as he continued running towards him.

Watching through the scope of his rifle, Deon felt a lump rise in his throat. *Come on, Sheila. Run out of the bunker ...*

The compound exploded in a blinding flash of light and thunder. The sheer force of the blast sent Simon flying through the air. Once the dust settled, Deon ran to him and helped him to his feet.

"You all right?" he asked anxiously.

"Fine," Simon said.

Deon knew he was lying, not because of the blood on his clothes, but by a look in his eye, he had rarely seen.

"Sheila's gone. Counselor Black killed her," said Simon, he couldn't believe the words and yet he was saying them.

The words hit Deon like a sledgehammer. He had known Sheila for years. Gone just like that. He almost fell backward from the shock.

"And Black?" Deon asked, rage building.

"Dead." Simon shook himself and wiped his face.

"Come on, that blast will attract company," said Simon.

They would grieve their shared loss later on friendlier, calmer soil. For now, they must run. They headed for the clearing where the truck and soldiers had been, praying the truck remained. Behind them, the muffled sounds of vehicles told them that the explosion was being investigated already.

The truck was still there. They hid in the surrounding bushes, waiting. The smell of cigarette smoke came from the other side of the truck.

"Tango, other side" whispered Simon as he stood up.

Deon knew instantly what he was going to do.

"No, you wait here." He put his hand on Simon's shoulder.

Simon could no longer ignore the pain from the fight and the explosion; he nodded in understanding. Deon crept quietly out of the bushes and walked towards the truck.

Close now, he drew his knife – no sense alerting nearby patrols with gunfire. Walking to the back of the truck, he peeked around. The guard was leaning against the truck with an AK-74 strapped across his back. Deon took a few seconds to aim; with a quick snap of his wrist, he threw the knife, hitting the guard in the neck. Deon then moved around into view, giving Simon a thumbs-up.

Simon tried not to think about Sheila as he picked up the guard's gun and slung it over his shoulder. As he got in the truck, he noticed the bodies of the men the soldiers had killed. *Should we have saved them? Was Sheila's death karma because we didn't?* Simon put such thoughts out of his mind; questions like those could kill as certainly as a bullet.

Luckily, the key was still in the ignition. Deon turned it, hoping that the stereotype about Russian trucks being crap wouldn't prove to be true.

The engine stuttered twice. Both men sighed with relief as it growled to life, lurching forward as Deon pointed it towards a dirt road on the other side of the clearing. From Connors' map, they knew it led to main roads, to the border, to home.

Chapter 20
Elegy

They hated funerals, reminders of comrades lost in battle. No strangers to death on the battlefield, they had grown sadly accustomed to it. For Sheila, though, they would make an exception.

The funeral was in her home town of Philadelphia, Pennsylvania. Simon, Deon, Connors, and Eduardo were the only ones in attendance, typical of the profession.

"Can't believe it's just us," Deon said.

"Her parents died years ago, she didn't have any family," explained Simon.

"I can't believe she didn't get a 21-gun salute or something," Eduardo said. "She pretty much saved the planet."

"It's what she would have wanted. Nothing flashy, just her brothers-in-arms saying one last goodbye. She told me that once. A long time ago." Simon's voice broke as he said the words despite his best attempts to hide it.

"She was one of the best," Connors said.

Simon brushed away a tear. "Damn right."

It had been a short graveside service, tasteful and quiet. The minister had left already; the four men stood looking blankly across the cemetery.

"So … what now? Do we just move on like this never happened?" Deon shook his head.

"Hell no!" Simon said, echoing all their thoughts.

"You're both welcome to stay with Silhouette," Connors said.

"Unfortunately, we have nothing on the Networc. It's as if they disappeared." Eduardo sounded defeated, but not vanquished entirely. "We'll keep looking." While Eduardo wasn't a field agent, he had worked with Sheila and the team. He was as outraged and confused as the rest of them. "We'll come up with something eventually. We have to."

"I've tasked all of Silhouette's agents across the world to find them," Connors said. "So far, nothing, but we won't stop."

Considering Silhouette's vast intelligence gathering resources, this was the height of frustration. Most infuriating of all was that one of their own had died by the Networc's hand and they knew nothing about the men behind her killer.

Simon looked up from Sheila's grave to Connors with an angry look. "You're giving them far too much credit. The Networc's just like all the terrorists and psychotics we've fought before. They'll go down the same way, too. I'll make *damn* sure of that," he retorted.

"You're making this personal," Deon said, noticing the change in Simon's tone. "You know that's dangerous."

Ever since their return to the States, where he and Sheila had wanted to rebuild a life together, Simon's grief had been supplanted with rage, with the burning desire for revenge.

Simon turned to Deon. "No. *They* made it personal when they killed Sheila. And they'll burn for it. Every last one of them," he growled.

Connors put his hand on Simon's shoulder. "I know what she meant to you," he cautioned, "but if you go down that path I won't have a choice. I'll have to send Blacklist Protocol after you and – "

Before he could finish, Simon swung around and hit him with a hard right punch in the jaw knocking Connors on the ground.

Deon and Eduardo said nothing, but they were not surprised. They had seen the rage building in Simon until it had to explode.

"Understand this, Connors – you don't know a fucking thing. They killed the only woman I ever loved, right in front of me," Simon growled. "Anyone or anything you throw at me will only be one more obstacle between me and them!" yelled Simon.

He had nothing else to say. Simon headed for his car, parked along the edge of the cemetery.

"Hey, Simon!" Deon yelled after him.

"If you need any help, call me!" barked Deon.

Simon paused before getting in his rental car and smiled.

"You got it," he called. *At least there's somebody I can count on.* He started the car and drove away, caring no more about his immediate destination than anyone could guess.

Eduardo helped Connors to his feet. "Damn, I was afraid of this," muttered Connors.

"To be fair, did you really think you could change his mind?" Deon asked, his eyes following Simon's car until it was out of sight.

Connors was grim as he brushed off his jacket and pants.

"Doesn't matter. Retired or not, he's a rogue asset with that attitude. Blacklist Protocol will take him down."

Deon suddenly realized that this might be the last time he'd ever see his friend again. Still ... if there was one man who could avoid being killed by Blacklist Protocol agents, it was Simon.

"So. Deon. What about you? Are you coming back or not?" Connors asked.

"Nah," Deon shook his head. "Without Simon and Sheila, there's no ECHO 9. And without ECHO 9, there's no point," answered Deon.

Connors grunted, understanding. The men all shook hands and went their separate ways.

*****

As Simon drove through the streets of Philadelphia, he pondered his next move. If a retired Silhouette agent leaves the country, he's hunted down and killed by Silhouette's lethal Internal Affairs division, known as Blacklist Protocol. However, he mused, as effective and dangerous as Blacklist Protocols agents were, it generally took 24 hours for orders to be processed and for agents to mobilize. *I'd have a head start. But I don't have a clue where to look.* So engrossed was he in his thoughts that he didn't notice the song playing on the radio, it was *Crimson and Clover by Joan Jett.* There song, the one played at their wedding.

As the song played he pulled into a parking lot and began to cry as he realized the reality that he would have to live in a world without her from now on. He rested his head on the steering wheel unable to hold the tears back anymore as the chorus played on over and over.

Suddenly he remembered the man that had first told them about the Networc. If anyone could provide him with information, it would be the inscrutable Mr. Bai. Simon sat up and wiped his tears on his sleeve, knowing what he had to do.

The problem with asking a gangster like him for help, of course, is that they usually expected something in return. He decided to risk asking a devil to help him, if it would lead to the capture of another. He reached into his coat pockets for his cellphone and the card. Finding Bai's card, he entered the number into his phone.

After a few rings, Bai picked up. "Hello, who is this?"

"Mr. Bai," Simon began respectfully, "I'm not sure if you remember but we met a few days ago … almost a week. I was with Deon Bowman."

Bai recognized Simon's voice instantly. "Ah yes, hello, Mr. ... MONOLITH, was it?"

Simon let out a silent breath. "Yes, Mr. Bai. I would like to ask a favor."

Bai made a humming noise. "All favors come with a price Mr. MONOLITH,"

"Name it," he replied.

"We both know that MONOLITH is not your real name. It is a code name assigned to you by your superiors. I wish to know what your real name is," said Bai.

Simon knew that Connors and Silhouette would be listening in on this conversation; likely, he would pay for his answer with his life, however he didn't care. All that mattered was making sure that Sheila's murderers died by his hand. "My name is Simon Kane," he replied.

Bai sniffed, satisfied. "Thank you, Mr. Kane. Ask your favor."

"I want a lead on the Networc," Simon said.

Bai made an appreciative sound. Mr. Kane had risked everything for what he considered to be a worthy piece of information.

"The Networc is hard for even us to find. Nevertheless, we believe they have an agent in Bangkok named Stanislaw."

Simon sensed that that was all Bai had, or was willing to share.

"Thank you," he said before hanging up.

Simon snapped the phone in half, lowered the window, and tossed it out the car window into traffic. He pulled out of the parking lot and stopped briefly at a department store for luggage and clothes before driving to Philadelphia International.

Simon gazed at the skyline with a little more appreciation than usual. At the airport, he booked a seat on the first one-way flight to Suvarnabhumi Airport in Thailand he could arrange.

With forty-five minutes till the plane took off, he walked to a Dunkin Donuts® and bought a chocolate frosted doughnut with sprinkles and a large coffee. He noticed a magazine rack nearby. The cover photo on top took his breath away. Pulling the issue out, he turned to the headline of the story inside.

"Sheila Goodbody dead: Famed thriller novelist and author of The Action Hero Squad *killed in a car accident."*

A car accident was the best death Silhouette could come up with for her.

He almost bought the magazine but decided against it. The world knew her as a writer of thriller novels, but he knew the real Sheila. He had no time for a cover story concocted by Silhouette. *More lies.*

On the wall, a TV showed CNN. Simon wasn't listening to it as he finished his snack, but when a word caught his eye, he read the news feed at the bottom of the screen.

"Mysterious explosion at Belarusian military bunker as peace talks between government forces and rebels enter third day. UN negotiators optimistic about conflict ending soon."

Silhouette was frighteningly good at creating cover stories. It irritated him how everything that had happened in Belarus was so casually swept under the rug. He had learned to live with that sad fact a long time ago, but this was different, still protocols were protocols.

Simon picked up his suitcase and walked to the terminal. After going through airport security and checking his suitcase, he boarded the plane. He had a window seat, thankfully.

As the plane took off, Simon leaned against the glass and closed his eyes, instantly falling asleep, dreaming of a beautiful woman with white pants and a black jacket, dancing to The Clash.

She was smiling right at him.

*Simon Kane's quest for vengeance continues
in book two of the Shadow World:
Edge of the Abyss*